When Dirk stepped into the kitchen, he stopped at the sight that met him. He had the feeling that he'd stepped into an old Christmas movie.

Singing to the soft Christmas music playing on the mounted-under-the-counter player, Abby had on an apron that had Mr and Mrs Claus kissing under a sprig of mistletoe on the front. She was stirring mixture in a glass bowl, and a whimsical smile played on her lips as she swayed to the beat of "Rocking Around the Christmas Tree". She looked happy. As if she belonged in this house, with its hand-me-down decorations and cozy holiday atmosphere.

Not that he found any of this cozy.

Only there was something about Abby that made him feel warmth where only coldness had resided for so long. There was also something about her that made him want to hold mistletoe over her head and kiss her.

He'd need a thatch hut with a mistletoe roof over her head to justify all the places he wanted to kiss Abby Arnold...

Dear Reader

Some of my favourite memories are of my children waking up on Christmas morning— of seeing their faces as they first catch sight of the goodies beneath the tree, of their laughter as they tear into packages, of watching the excitement in their eyes. Other wonderful memories are of going to my parents', sampling my mom's homemade goodies, enjoying time with my rather large extended family, looking around and seeing people treat others with love and generosity, making an extra effort to make the world a better place for others. All those things are what make up Christmas, but other not so happy memories can hit hard at the holidays as well. Memories of loved ones who are no longer with us, in particular.

In THE NURSE WHO SAVED CHRISTMAS I wanted to capture the warmth of the holidays, but also the pain of when your heart's not whole. Abby and Dirk have to learn the true meaning of the holidays, and of love. I hope you enjoy their story, and that you have a wonderful Christmas filled with all the magic of the season.

I love to hear from readers. Please e-mail me at Janice@janicelynn.net, write to me care of Harlequin Mills & Boon, or visit me at my website: www.janicelynn.net

Janice Lynn

THE NURSE WHO SAVED CHRISTMAS

BY
JANICE LYNN

First published in Great Britain 2010
by Mills & Boon,
an imprint of Harlequin (UK) Limited,
Large Print edition 2011
Eton House, 18-24 Paradise Road,
Richmond, Surrey TW9 1SR

© Janice Lynn 2010

ISBN: 978 0 263 21743 8

Harlequin (UK) policy is to use papers that are
natural, renewable and recyclable products and made
from wood grown in sustainable forests. The logging
and manufacturing process conform to the legal
environmental regulations of the country of origin.

Printed and bound in Great Britain
by CPI Antony Rowe, Chippenham, Wiltshire

Janice Lynn has a Masters in Nursing from Vanderbilt University, and works as a nurse practitioner in a family practice. She lives in the southern United States with her husband, their four children, their Jack Russell—appropriately named Trouble—and a lot of unnamed dust bunnies that have moved in since she started her writing career. To find out more about Janice and her writing, visit www.janicelynn.com

Recent titles by the same author:

OFFICER, GENTLEMAN…SURGEON!
DR DI ANGELO'S BABY BOMBSHELL
PLAYBOY SURGEON, TOP-NOTCH DAD
THE PLAYBOY DOCTOR CLAIMS HIS BRIDE
SURGEON BOSS, SURPRISE DAD

To my children, who bring Christmas alive
and are life's greatest gifts. I love you.

CHAPTER ONE

NURSE ABBY ARNOLD hid her smile behind her hand as Santa Claus grimaced at the squirming kid sitting in his lap at the children's advocacy Christmas community outreach in downtown Philadelphia.

"Smile for the picture," she said sweetly, standing a few feet from the elaborate thronelike chair and Christmas tree being used for "Pictures with Santa."

Santa Claus's deep blue eyes narrowed behind his gold-rimmed glasses, but his lips curved in a smile hopefully only she could tell was forced.

How had she talked Dr. Dirk Kelley into helping when the Santa she'd arranged for the event canceled at the last minute, leaving her desperate for a replacement? So desperate she'd asked a man she'd treated as if they were just friendly colleagues for the past two months and not more, all the while walking on eggshells at the sharp undercurrents between them.

"Ho, ho, ho, what do you want for Christmas this year, little boy?" Santa asked, sounding more like the Abominable Snowman than a jolly old man full of Christmas spirit.

Despite her awkward physical awareness of the man beneath the suit, it was all Abby could do not to snort. Did Dirk really believe that voice sounded Santa-ish? Hadn't he sat on Santa's knee as a kid? Watched Christmas television shows about jolly Saint Nick? Anything that would clue him in that Christmas was the most magical time of the year and that for these kids he was part of that magic? Something they'd always remember?

For all she knew, he hadn't.

Although they'd started out with a bang the night they'd first worked together, she really didn't know much about the handsome doctor who'd knocked her socks off from the moment she'd met him.

She knew very little about him or his past. Although, thanks to *that* morning, she spent way too much of her present thinking about him and how much she'd like to feature in his future.

The kid on Dirk's lap, around five, wiped the back of his pudgy hand across his runny nose. "An Xbox, and a cellphone, and a digital voice enhancer, and a…"

The list went on. And on. Even Abby's eyes widened at some of the items the kid listed. What had happened to a baseball glove or a bicycle?

Santa's bushy white brow rose as he regarded the kid. "Have you been that good this year?"

Another wipe of the face, then a nod. "I have. Extra-good."

"I'll see what I can do." At the mother's frantic look, Santa diplomatically added, "But Santa's on a budget. To be fair to the other good little boys and girls, I'll have to prioritize and just bring one or two of your list items."

The mother heaved a relieved sigh.

Santa set the boy off his lap but, rather than walk away, the kid wrapped his arms around

Dirk's neck and planted a noisy kiss on a high cheekbone Abby had doctored earlier with rosy rouge. "I love you, Santa."

Abby's insides melted. How sweet! This was why she'd volunteered to organize this event. Why she volunteered with so many Christmas events. To help bring holiday magic alive for others.

Only Dirk looked more like he was being cooked alive than feeling the magic.

"I…uh…" His eyes cut to her with a distressed plea for rescue. He didn't have to say anything aloud. Abby got the message loud and clear.

Not in a million years could she deny him. Not when his gaze held hers and she had a resurgence of the connection she'd instantaneously felt with him, had a resurgence of the connection they'd shared *that* morning. One so real, so tangible, she'd felt in sync with him, had comforted and been comforted.

No, she couldn't deny Dirk much of anything within her power to give. Obviously. Besides, she was good at helping others, giving to others. It's what she did. What she'd always done. What was expected of her by all who knew her, especially this time of year.

Wondering at Dirk's evident rising unease, she put her hand on the boy's back and gave him a gentle pat. "Santa loves you, too. Don't forget to keep being extra-good between now and Christmas. He'll be watching."

At the last, the kid shot a wary glance toward Santa, his face contorting in shock. "Even when I'm in the bathtub?"

"No, not then. Just when you're being good or bad." Sending an apologetic smile, the boy's mother took his hand and led him away. Several times he glanced over his shoulder, waving goodbye.

Standing to tower above her five feet, six inches, Dirk bent to whisper in her ear. "Santa needs a break. Stat."

His rush of warm breath tickling her ear filled her with Christmas magic, from her head to the tippy-tips of her toes. This so wasn't the place to be getting hot and bothered by Dirk and his overabundant male magnetism.

In a Santa costume, for goodness' sake.

How could she possibly be turned on by a man dressed in her deceased father's treasured Santa suit? Although she loved Christmas, she wasn't prone to Christmas fetishes. Then again, it wasn't the suit but the man inside it lighting up her world like the most overdecorated house in the neighborhood.

He was playing Santa as a favor to her—she had no choice but to get her feelings under control and not attack the man's lips with hers in front of all these children.

She gave a calm nod and told the waiting crowd, "Sorry, kids, but Santa needs to check in with his elves to make sure all the toys are being made just right." She smiled brilliantly at the children and their parents. "We'll be back in ten minutes."

As expected, moans and groans greeted them from the families in the long line. Despite Dirk's obvious need for a reprieve, she sensed his hesitation, liked him all the more for it. Still, he'd said he needed a break and she'd seen in his eyes that he really did.

"Come on, Santa." Smiling brightly, Abby looped her arm in a red-velvet-covered one and spoke loudly. "Follow me, and I'll take you to where you can use your special Santa phone to call the North Pole and put in the requests for presents you've heard so far. There's only two more weeks until Christmas, so they need to get started filling the orders right away."

Gratitude shining in his eyes, Dirk nodded, pasted on a fake smile, and waved at the crowd.

"I can't believe I let you talk me into this," he mumbled under his breath while allowing her to lead him away from the masses gathered at the community center just to meet him. "This is madness. Pure commercialized madness."

She still couldn't believe he'd said yes, either. Sure, he was the one man capable of delivering her Christmas wish, but long and lean Dr. Dirk Kelley playing the role of Santa to dozens of children was another matter altogether. They'd worked together long enough for her to realize kids made him uncomfortable, that he was quiet and kept to himself. Her friend and fellow nurse Danielle called him Dr. Dreamboat. Abby called him what she most wanted for Christmas, but had never said the words out loud, not even to her tabby cat, Mistletoe.

Regardless, Dirk was doing her a huge favor and she was grateful. Smiling, she quirked a brow in his direction. "Ah, Santa, where's your Christmas spirit?"

He snorted. "I lost it somewhere between demands for a new computer and the kid who wanted a Mercedes-Benz." He shook his red and white hat and white wig topped head in dismay. "What happened to kids wanting Tinkertoys and tricycles?"

Although he pretty much echoed her earlier thoughts, Abby just shrugged. "Now, Santa, stay with the times. It's high tech and electronics these days. You'll have to get your elves with the program."

"Apparently," he said wryly. The moment they stepped out of the main walkway of the community center and into the privacy of the employee break room where they'd left their things earlier, his broad shoulders sagged. "I'm not sure I'm going to last another hour. Christmas just isn't my thing, Abs."

"Bah, humbug, Mr. Scrooge." While trying to decide if he was serious about the Christmas comment, she gave an internal sigh at his use of his pet name for her. Did he have any idea how that sent shivers through her? That every time she heard it she was instantly taken back to being in his arms, to the first time he'd whispered the name when they'd been tangled together beneath her bedsheets? "Surely you can make it another hour." She sighed theatrically. "Guess men of endurance are a thing of the past, too."

"Don't you believe it," he warned, grinning for real for the first time in over an hour, his eyes taking on a dangerous gleam despite his costume and obvious dislike of his role. "My endurance is just fine. Better than fine."

She raked her gaze over his red fur-covered body. The padding beneath the suit didn't begin to hide the wide shoulders and abundant male charisma. Not really. Abby had caught more than one mom in line eyeing Santa as if they'd like to sit on his knee and ask for him in their Christmas stockings… If they knew Santa was none other than scrumptious Dr. Dirk Kelley, Santa would have had to beat the women off with a giant candy cane.

Besides, thanks to the particularly rough night they'd first worked together, Abby did know all about Dirk's endurance. If only she could forget what amazing stamina the man wielded at the tips of those magical fingers. What stamina the rest of him had delivered. Twice.

Dirk Kelley didn't need a sleigh and flying reindeer to take a woman to soaring heights.

Maybe somebody should thwack *her* with a giant candy cane for even letting memories of *that* morning creep into her thoughts. Hadn't they agreed they'd made a mistake? Memories like those could only cause her to want to sit on

Santa's lap and tell him what she'd like to find under her tree on Christmas morning.

And that was a family.

Kids anxiously waiting to rip into brightly colored packages.

Aunts, uncles, cousins, parents and grandparents to fuss and carry on about everything from setting the table for Christmas morning breakfast to who was the most surprised by their gift.

A man to share her life with, to love her, and surprise her with something special just for her. Not necessarily something expensive, just something with meaning, something from his heart.

Like the beloved Christmas village pieces her father used to give to her mother before they'd been killed in a house fire when Abby had been seven. She wanted to experience what her parents had shared, to open a package and glance up with excitement, not at the physical gift but with the love with which it had been chosen. She wanted to see that love reflected back at her in the glow of twinkling Christmas morning lights.

But on top of all that, she wanted Dirk.

Abby sighed.

Other than her very busy volunteer schedule and long work hours, Abby led a lonely life. Oh, she had friends, lots of friends, amazing friends like Danielle, but she didn't have someone to come home to, someone to whom she was the most important person in their life, someone to love and be loved by. Only her tabby cat Mistletoe cared whether or not she came home in the mornings after working the emergency department night shift.

Oblivious to her onset of melancholy, Dirk adjusted his belly padding, scratched at his glued-on beard. "I'll never complain about a monkey suit again. After this getup, wearing a tuxedo will feel like a real treat."

Pulling herself from her unwanted self-pitying thoughts and trying not to think about how handsome Dirk would look in a tux, *out of a tux*, Abby focused on the here and now. She had a great life, a great job and great friends. She was a needed, productive member of society. At the moment she was needed to give downtown Philadelphia children a magical visit with Santa.

Abby wasn't the kind of woman to disappoint. Not when she had any say in the matter and never when it came to children and Christmas.

"Better let me adjust your beard there, Santa." She tugged on Dirk's fake white beard, soothing down the coarse lifelike hair he'd ruffled with his scratching.

Just touching him prickled her skin with goose bumps.

Glancing everywhere but at her, he fanned his face. "Man, this thing is hot."

He was what was hot. Hot as a roaring fire she'd like to warm herself next to. Oh, my! Abby turned away before she had to fan her face, too.

"You think that's why Santa's cheeks stay red?" She reached into the break room's refrigerator and pulled out a cold bottle of water.

"I thought it was from kissing all the mommies under the mistletoe," he surprised her by saying.

Abby blinked at him, at how the corners of his mouth hitched upward ever so slightly. Was he flirting with her?

Laughing a bit nervously, she handed him the water. "Well, there is that."

Twisting off the top and taking a long swig, Dirk sagged into a chair, his blue gaze lifting to hers. "Tell me I don't really have to go back out there."

"You don't have to, but you will, anyway."

He would, too. In the short time since he'd arrived in Philadelphia, just a couple of weeks prior to Halloween, Dirk had proved himself the type of man who didn't shirk a commitment. Even one he so obviously regretted having made. Why had he? Guilt at what had happened between them? At his hasty retreat into "This never should have happened" immediately afterward? She'd hid her hurt. She knew she had. And she'd told herself she should be relieved—workplace romances never seemed to end well.

"You're right." Even for a guy dressed like Santa Claus his sigh was a bit too melodramatic.

"I will, but you owe me, Abs. Big-time. Any time. Any place. Any thing. You owe me. Take note."

Despite how her heart tattooed a funky beat at his unexpected words, wondering if maybe that morning haunted him, too, Abby placed her hands on her hips. Or maybe it was because of his words she felt the need to stand her ground. "I think 'any' is a bit too general."

"Nope." He shook his Santafied head. "Any it is."

She sighed. How bad could owing him be? They'd both agreed falling into bed together had been a mistake, the result of a particularly bad night in the E.R. where three people had died due to trauma received in a multicar accident. Although they'd done everything medically possible, the internal injuries had been too extensive. An elderly man had suffered a heart attack and hit another car head-on. He'd died instantly, but a two-year-old girl and her mother had been alive, barely, when paramedics had rushed them into the emergency room. The mother had died within minutes, the child soon thereafter. Abby's heart had felt ripped out by shift change. Surprisingly, Dirk had been just as devastated. It had been the only time she'd seen his E.R. physician armor crack.

They'd ended up at her house, clinging to each other for comfort. That's all *that* morning had been. Comfort sex between two normal, healthy adults who found each other attractive.

Not that comfort sex with Dirk had been a bad thing. She supposed sex with any man of his probable experience would be fabulous. Definitely, Dirk had been fabulous. Practice made perfect, right?

Which meant there was no way his any thing, any time, any place would have anything to do with a repeat performance. He might have been well on his way to the perfect lover, but she'd been sorely lacking in practice.

As in a couple of not-so-perfect boyfriends.

So why had she asked Dirk in when he'd dropped her by her house when he'd caught her crying in the elevator and insisted on driving her home? How had him walking her to her front door ended with him carrying her to her bedroom, stripping her naked, and initiating her to the joys shared between a man and a woman that up to that point she'd only believed happened in romance novels?

"Abs?" He pulled her back to the present.

She blinked again, hoping more fervently than every kid on Christmas Eve that he couldn't read her thoughts.

He pushed the gold-rimmed glasses back against the straight slant of his nose. "Do we have a deal?"

She may as well agree. It wasn't as if Dirk would ever really need anything from her. He was gorgeous, and despite his grumblings about having to play the role of Santa, Dirk was good-hearted, an honorable man and an excellent doctor. The physical chemistry between them kept her from being a hundred percent comfortable in his presence—how could she be comfortable when she looked at him and remembered how delicious his kisses tasted, how his naked body felt gliding against hers?

Just thinking about him made her feel a little giddy. There was always a little extra bounce to her step on the nights her shift overlapped his emergency room duties.

"Fine." She met his gaze and wondered what he was up to. The man was brilliant. He was also the only Santa she had. She needed him. "For the kids. I owe you."

"Good," he said, standing. "Let's get this over with."

Dirk's smile scared her. Which felt wrong. How could a smiling Santa be intimidating? Yet, as his gloved hand clasped hers, her nervous system lit up like a twinkling Christmas tree.

CHAPTER TWO

FROM the moment his precious two-year-old daughter and his wife had been killed in a car accident on their way to an early-morning Christmas bargain sale, Dirk Kelley had hated Christmas.

He'd avoided anything to do with the holiday year after year. To the point that his family had held a well-intended but unnecessary intervention at last year's not-so-joyous festivities.

After their unwelcome confrontation, telling him he needed to deal with Sandra and Shelby's deaths, they'd continued to hound him, to try to set him up on dates, to beg him to live life. By early summer, he'd known he had to move away from Oak Park, where his family resided, before the next holiday season. Much to their disappointment, he'd accepted the job in Philadelphia, knowing he was far enough away to avoid holiday get-togethers and their piteous look, but not so far away that he couldn't make it home if there was an emergency. He loved them, just couldn't deal with the pity in their eyes, their interference in what was left of his life.

They were wrong. He hadn't needed the intervention. What he'd needed was for his wife and daughter to be alive, but that was impossible. He'd accepted that inevitability years ago, accepted that he had to move on with his life, and he had. But that didn't mean he'd ever want to be involved with another woman or would welcome the month of December and all the holiday hoopla that arrived with it.

If he could fast-forward December, he'd gladly do so. The lights, the smells, the sales, the noises, everything about the month ripped open his never-healing chest wound.

Abby's initial shocked expression must have mirrored his own when he'd agreed to be her Santa.

Mortification and panic had struggled for top

seat. Yet he hadn't been able to take back his ill-fated yes. Not when the wariness she'd eyed him with since the morning after they'd met had finally disappeared, replaced with surprise and soft hazel-eyed gratitude. That look had done something to his insides. Something strange and foreign and despite knowing how difficult today was going to be, he hadn't retracted his agreement.

Not when doing so would disappoint Abby.

Thank God the deed was behind him and he could put Christmas nonsense behind him, where it belonged.

Thankfully de-Santafied, he wandered around Abby's living room. The room had been taken hostage by Christmas Past since the last time he'd been here, two months ago. He'd swear he'd stepped into a nostalgic Christmas movie scene from a couple of decades ago.

An ancient wreath hung over Abby's fireplace, a slightly thinning silver garland was draped over a doorway with faded red ribbons marking each corner. A small Christmas village complete with fake glittery snow and dozens of tiny trees and villagers was set up on a white cloth-covered table, clearly set up in a place of honor beside the tree. The nine main pieces of the village looked old, expensive.

Her live Christmas tree towered almost to the ceiling, a ceramic-faced angel's tinsel halo mere inches from it. What a crazy tradition. Trees indoors. The entire room smelt like the pine tree—like Christmas. Smells he didn't like. Smells that haunted him and took him to hellish places he didn't want to go.

There had been a Christmas tree in the waiting room of the emergency department the morning Sandra and Shelby had died. Amazing how the smell could take him back to sitting in that room, a broken man, a doctor who hadn't been able to do a damned thing to save his baby girl and her mother.

He walked over to the fireplace, eyeing the giant painted toy soldiers to each side, picking up a slightly worn wooden nutcracker. He shook his head, waiting for the nausea to hit him, waiting for the cold sweat to cover his skin, the grief to bring him to his knees.

Christmas did that to him. Sure, he'd learned to bury his pain beneath what most labeled as cynicism, but that didn't mean in private moments the past didn't sneak up to take a stab through his armor, to chip away another piece of what was left of him.

And yet, for the first time since Sandra and Shelby's deaths, he'd agreed to do something that fed into the whole commercialism of Christmas. All because pretty little nurse Abby Arnold had asked him. She'd lit up so brilliantly someone could stick a halo on her head and place her on top of a tree.

He'd definitely found a piece of heaven on earth in her arms. Had found solace he hadn't expected in the heat of her kisses.

Solace? After the first sweep of his mouth over her lush lips, he hadn't been seeking comfort but acting on the attraction he'd instantly felt for the pretty brunette nurse. He'd been on fire. With lust. With need. With the desire to be inside her curvy body.

He hadn't been remembering or forgetting. He'd been in the moment. With Abby.

He'd wanted her the second he'd laid eyes on her, but never had he experienced such all-consuming sex as that morning. So all-consuming he'd known they couldn't repeat it. Quite easily he could see himself getting obsessed with having her body wrapped around him, getting serious when he had no intention of ever having another serious relationship. Just look at how often he thought of Abby and they'd only had the one morning where they'd made love, twice, and collapsed into exhausted sleep.

Letting out a slow, controlled breath, Dirk placed the nutcracker back on her mantel. Any time, any place, any thing. Why had he teased her into making such an outlandish promise? Better yet, why had he asked for what he had?

He turned, planning to go and find Abby, to tell her he'd changed his mind and needed to go.

A fat tabby cat in a wicker basket at the end

of the sofa caught his eye. They'd been formally introduced when the cat had jumped onto the bed, waking both Dirk and Abby in the middle of the afternoon that mid-October day. The cat had been observing his perusal of the room but other than watch him with boredom the cat never moved except to close its eyes.

Realizing another smell, one that was making his stomach grumble, was taking precedence over the pine and was coming through an open doorway, he followed his nose.

When he stepped into the kitchen, he stopped still at the sight that met him, wondering if he'd had one too many kids call him Santa. Because he certainly had the feeling that he'd stepped into an old Christmas movie again.

Singing to the soft Christmas music playing on the mounted under-the-counter player, Abby had on an apron that had Mr. and Mrs. Claus kissing under a sprig of mistletoe on the front. She'd pulled her thick hair back with a red ribbon and had kicked off her shoes for a pair of worn, fuzzy Rudolph slippers.

Stirring a mixture in a glass bowl, a whimsical smile played on her lips as she swayed to the beat of "Rocking Around the Christmas Tree." She looked happy. Like she belonged in this house with its hand-me-down decorations and cozy holiday atmosphere.

Not that he found any of this cozy.

Only there was something about Abby that made him feel warmth where only coldness had resided for so long. There was also something about her that made him want to hold mistletoe over her head and kiss her.

He'd need a thatched hut with a mistletoe roof over her head to justify all the places he wanted to kiss Abby Arnold.

He wanted to do more than kiss her. Lots more. Like take some of that fudge and smear it across her…

Her gaze lifting from the glass bowl she held, she smiled, knocking the breath from his lungs with her beauty and sincerity. "I can't believe you wanted home-made fudge as your any time, any place, any thing."

Her smile said he'd pleased her with his ravings about the goodies she'd brought to the break room at the hospital and how he wanted another bite.

He wanted another bite all right.

Her dimples dug a little deeper into her lovely face. "Some men are so easy."

Smiling at him like that, she made him feel easy. Like he was cookie dough in her hands, waiting for her to mold him into whatever shape she wanted. So why was he still there? Why hadn't he told her he was leaving as he'd come in here to do?

Why was he smiling back at her? Why was he eyeing the pan of chocolate-chip cookies she'd taken out of the oven and feeling a pang of hunger in his belly? A pang that didn't begin to compare to the one below his belt caused by eyeing Abby.

"If they've tasted your homemade goodies, I understand why. Especially the peanut-butter fudge."

"Thank you." Her eyes sparkled like the silver

tinsel draping her tree. "It was my mother's recipe."

"Was?"

A flicker of pain crossed her face. "She died."

"I'm sorry." He was. Death was never easy. If anyone knew that, he did. In spades. No, death wasn't easy. Not even when you were a highly trained doctor who'd been dealing with life and death on a daily basis for years.

Just look at how stupidly he'd behaved that first night he and Abby had worked together. Even now, his reaction to the motor vehicle accident victims bothered him, but he understood why, understood that when he'd been battling to save the mother and daughter, he'd been trying to save his wife, trying to save Shelby.

Only to fail.

But he'd held up fine, wearing the mask he'd perfected in those months following their deaths. Pretending he was okay when inside all he'd felt was cold.

Until he'd run into Abby.

He'd been on his way out of the hospital, had

caught the elevator just as the door had started closing, and been startled to see a red-eyed Abby eyeing him in surprise.

After shift change, she'd obviously slipped into the bathroom and had a good cry, was still fighting tears. She'd looked vulnerable, needy, way too distraught to be getting behind the wheel of a car.

Way too distraught for him to let her.

He'd insisted on driving her home.

Which was all fine and dandy.

Walking her to the door, going inside, staying, was where he'd messed up.

He didn't date hospital employees, wouldn't date hospital employees.

He hadn't really dated Abby. He'd just not been able to stand the sadness in her eyes, to stand the thought of her driving upset and possibly something happening to her. They'd ended up naked, in her bed, making love until they'd both collapsed in each other's arms and slept the day away.

He shouldn't have done that.

Shouldn't have agreed to be her Santa.

Shouldn't be here now.

So why was he pulling up a chair, willingly staying somewhere Christmas tunes played, instead of beating a path to the door?

Was her imagination running wild or was Dirk looking at her like he'd rather take a bite out of her instead of the peanut-butter fudge?

Abby turned away from his intense blue eyes and took a deep breath. Needing to do something with her hands, she twisted on the faucet and filled the sink with sudsy water to wash the dishes she'd used to make the cookies and two batches of fudge—one chocolate, one peanut butter.

"This is really great."

There was no doubting the sincerity in his voice. She'd swear she heard him moan a moment ago.

Without turning toward him, Abby began stacking the dishes into the hot water to let them soak a few minutes.

"My mother had tons of great recipes, but…"
But most of them had been lost in the fire. Only
her mother's Christmas recipes packed away in
the crates in the basement had survived. The
items stored in the basement had been the only
items that had survived, period. Almost every
box had contained precious Christmas items. "I
always bring several big platters full of goodies
to the hospital every Christmas."

"Like the fudge you brought the other day?"

"That, and more." She grabbed a dish towel,
turned toward him and leaned against the sink.
"I like to bake. I like how the house smells when
I have cookies in the oven and candies going on
the stovetop and…"

Realizing she was probably boring him, heat
flushed her face. She wiped her hands more with
the dish towel, wondering if the moisture was
from the dishwater or from nervous clamminess.
Dirk made her edgy.

"Sorry." She smiled wryly. "Christmas is my favorite holiday and I get carried away at times."

"Obviously."

Despite the amusement in his eyes, something about the way he said the word struck her as wrong. "What's that supposed to mean?"

His grin stayed in place but, still, there was something off kilter, something a bit too brittle about him. "Just that it looks like Bing Crosby should be showing up any moment to start singing about a white Christmas."

"What would be so bad about that? He was a great singer. What's wrong with you anyway? All day you've acted like you really don't like Christmas."

He shrugged. "I don't."

"Say it isn't so!" Astounded, flabbergasted, shocked, her mouth dropped open and her palm flattened against her chest, dish towel and all.

"Why?" He shrugged, looking so serious it made Abby want to loosen her apron strings. "It's the truth. I'm surprised you buy into such a commercialized holiday."

"The business world commercializes every holiday but that doesn't lessen what the day is about."

"Which is?"

"Are you kidding me?" She eyed him, wondering if he was teasing her. When he'd first told her he didn't like Christmas, she'd thought he was just trying to get out of playing Santa. Could anyone really not like Christmas? Why wouldn't they? "Christmas is about everything good in life. It's a time when families come together and give of themselves to each other. A time when the world slows down and gives a helping hand to someone in need. It's—"

"It's a time when people run up credit-card debt they can't pay. It's a time of the highest rate of depression cases treated, the highest rate of suicide, the highest rate of—"

"How can you be such a cynic about Christmas?" Abby tossed the dish towel onto the countertop and frowned. How could someone not love Christmas? Not love the bright colors in the stores, the sounds of Christmas over the radio, the decorations along the streets? Abby even loved walking past the Salvation Army bellringers. Dropping money into their collection pails always made her feel warm and fuzzy inside.

Giving of oneself was the greatest joy of the holidays. Sure, it would be nice to have someone give to her, to share the moments with, but she'd already decided once today that she'd had enough self-pity.

"I'm not a cynic," he denied, but the more he talked, the more convinced she became that he was.

"I'm a realist," he clarified. "For most, Christmas is a major stressor with trying to come up with the perfect gift, trying to figure out how they're going to pay for that gift, and how they're going to fight the crowds to make sure they get their hands on that perfect gift."

"You're so negative," she pointed out, wondering what had given him such a slanted view of her favorite time of the year. "I see Christmas as at time when you get to search out that special gift to bring a smile to someone's face. A gift meant just for them from you that signifies who they are and how much you appreciate having them in your life."

"It's about rushing from one place to the next," he went on, as if she'd never interrupted his tirade. "Never quite satisfying family and friends with how much of your time you can allot for the festivities they planned without any consideration for your busy schedule. It's about high emotions and family bickering and—"

"Bah, humbug," she interrupted, pulling out a chair at the table and sitting down beside him, positive she was staring at a complete stranger. Who would have thought the wonderful emergency doctor was such a Scrooge? The caring man who'd been as devastated by the deaths of two patients as she had? "Say what you will, but that's not what Christmas is about. Not to me, and you should be ashamed for being so...so... Grinchy!"

He eyed her for long, silent moments, studying her as if she were an oddity. Then, as if he'd not just dissed her favorite holiday, dissed her favorite childhood memories of perfect Christmas moments, his lips curved into a crooked smile. "If it's any consolation, I really like Christmas fudge."

Taking a deep breath, relaxing the tension that had tightened her neck muscles, Abby sighed. How could she stay annoyed at him when he gave her that boyish look that made her toes curl in her shoes?

"Good thing I didn't know all this about you when I asked you to be Santa," she said, smoothing out the edge of a plain red and green table placemat. "You, Dr. Kelley, are no Santa Claus."

"You asked me to be Santa because you couldn't get anyone else to agree." Still showing wry amusement, his gaze pinned hers. "Admit it."

An unexpected giggle rose up her throat. "Okay, you're right. Everyone else I asked claimed to be busy."

"Such classic examples of Christmas goodwill and cheer."

"They were probably busy," she said defensively,

although she doubted any of them could match her holiday season schedule. Every year she took on as many projects as she could fit in.

"Sure they were." He popped the last piece of his fudge into his mouth. "But if they'd known they could maneuver their way into your kitchen, you'd have had to beat Santa-wannabes away with stockings filled with coal."

"I'm guessing you'd know a lot about those stockings filled with coal." At his mock look of horror, she smiled. "You should've tried my mother's Martha Washington candy."

Memories of standing on a chair beside her mother, carefully dipping rolled candies into melted chocolate, her mother smiling down at her, praising her efforts, filled Abby's heart. How she longed for a family to spend Christmas with.

Dirk reached for a second square of fudge. His sooty ashes swept across his cheeks as he bit into it. Was it shameful she'd like to see that blissful look on his face while he tasted her lips? Yes. Yes, it was. They'd agreed anything physical between them was a mistake. She'd agreed when he'd said that.

It had been a mistake. Hadn't it? Or had agreeing with him been the mistake?

Because looking at him, being here with him, denying the way she wanted him when she wanted him so badly sure felt like the bigger mistake.

CHAPTER THREE

"IF YOU'RE more into peanut butter, there's always peanut-butter balls and homemade peanut brittle," she rushed out, trying to redirect her mind away from the direction it was headed.

Eyes wide, his gaze lifted to hers. He looked like an eager little boy. *Like he'd looked that morning when he'd devoured her mouth.*

He placed his hand over his heart. "I've died and gone to heaven. You're right. I was too easy. I should have asked for peanut brittle."

She laughed out loud at his look of ecstasy.

Just as quickly her laughter faded as more memories of another time, another look of ecstasy had been on his handsome face.

When he'd been standing just inside her front door, awkwardly saying goodbye but making no move to leave. The only move he'd made had been to bend and gently kiss her lips.

Then he'd kissed her not so gently.

Oh, Lord, how he'd kissed her.

And kissed her.

No, she couldn't keep thinking of *that* morning. Not with him here, alone, in her house, just the two of them and the bed where he'd made love to her.

No, not love. They'd just been two colleagues dealing poorly with a very stressful night in the emergency room.

Her gaze tangled with his and his good humor faded just as quickly as hers had. Was he remembering, too? Recalling that the last time he'd been in her house, he'd never seen the kitchen but had had an up-close-and-personal tour of her bedroom?

He stuck the remainder of his fudge in his mouth, stood and brushed his hands over the faded jeans he'd changed into in her guest bathroom after his shower. When he'd swallowed the

mouthful, he took a step back. "I put your Santa
suit on the sofa."

His words managed to pull her from memories of Dirk's last visit to further in the past. Her
father's Santa suit. When Dirk had asked her
about what he'd wear, she'd instantly offered her
father's suit.

"Thanks for the fudge and for the loan of the
suit."

"It was the least I could do as you filled in for
Santa." True, but had anyone else agreed to play
the role, she would have bought a cheap Santa
costume from a department store. For Dirk, she'd
dug out the treasured suit that had belonged to
her father.

"Thanks all the same."

"If you hadn't agreed, I'd have had to play
Santa." Not that her father's suit would have
fit her, but she'd have made it work somehow.
"I think the kids might have been scarred for
life."

His gaze raked over the ample upper part of her
body. "You're probably right about that. You're

no Santa." He tossed her earlier words back at her.

Abby didn't know whether to be offended or flattered. Either way, heat crept into her face.

"I'll get a dish for you to take some home." She stood so rapidly her chair almost toppled. Pulling out a Christmas patterned storage tin, she placed a generous piece of plastic wrap inside, arranged as much as would fit of the fudge and cookies, and put the lid on. "There you go."

He'd moved over next to her, standing near the cabinets. His body heat radiated toward her, luring her nearer. "I feel guilty, coercing you to make this and then taking most of it."

"You should feel guiltier if you left it here," she teased a bit nervously, playfully elbowing him, the contact shooting stars through the pit of her belly.

His gaze dropped to where she'd touched his arm then his brow rose in question of her comment.

"If you left it, I'd eat it," she clarified, not lowering her gaze despite how her blood pumped through her body at warp speed and made her feel as if she needed to call time out so she could catch her breath.

Again his eyes ran over her features, taking their time and not seeming to mind the bumps and valleys along the journey. "That would be a bad thing?"

"I'm a woman who is constantly on a diet," she admitted, sucking in her waist reflexively as his gaze traveled lower. Not that holding her belly in would do much good.

"You have no reason to be on a diet." When his eyes met hers, they were blue fire, hot, lust-filled.

A thousand carolers began to sing in her soul, louder and louder until she might explode from the sheer beauty of it, until she was sure the sound must be able to be heard in heaven itself.

"No reason at all," he repeated, his gaze burning hotter. "You're perfect just as you are."

Um, right. Perfect. If you liked a woman who was busty and hippy, with a little extra thigh thrown in on the sides. But she couldn't look away from Dirk, because he was either the most talented fibber in the world or he meant what he said. And, darn, if those carolers hadn't gone up another octave in the pit of her belly, making every individual cell vibrate in a happy dance.

"I, uh…" What could she say when he was looking at her as if a slightly fuller figure really was perfection? She shoved the fudge at him. "Thank you, but I'm glad you're taking it, all the same."

He looked as if he wanted to say more, but must have decided against doing so as he took the candy, stared at her a few moments, his gaze going from fire to almost a sad smoldering. "Bye, Abs. You working tomorrow night?"

Abs. He really shouldn't say her name like that so carelessly! Holding her breath, she nodded.

"Are you planning to go to the hospital Christmas party this weekend?" Had he winced while asking that? Or after the words had left his mouth?

"Of course," she answered slowly, watching the play of conflicting emotions dance on his face.

"I'm on the hospital's Christmas committee and helped put the party together. Are you going?"

"I hadn't planned to, but…" He paused, looked as if he needed to loosen his collar even though his black T-shirt was far from restricting at the neck.

"But?" she prompted, her eyes focusing on a bead of sweat she'd swear was forming on his brow.

He took a deep breath, as if he was about to embark on a dangerous quest he really didn't want to go on but had little choice. "If you'll go with me, I could probably tolerate it this once. When I didn't RSVP, the hospital administrator came by." Dirk sighed, looking almost as uncomfortable as he had when he'd been playing Santa. "He said it wouldn't look good for the newest member on the medical staff to not show for the hospital's biggest employee social event of the year."

Not the most enthusiastic invitation she'd ever received, but happiness spread through Abby.

Dirk had just asked her on a date to the hospital Christmas party.

Not that he really wanted to go, but he'd asked her to accompany him. On a date.

"I'd love to go to the Christmas party with you." There wasn't a man alive she'd rather attend with. Being at Dirk's side would make the party all the more special, made everything all the more special.

Would he please turn around a moment so she could happy-dance around the kitchen?

Dirk had asked her to the Christmas party! Their morning hadn't been a one-night stand after all. Er…a one-morning stand after all.

"Okay. Great." He sounded relieved at her answer.

Had he thought she'd say no or was it the Christmas party itself stressing him? Either way, Dirk had just asked her to go on a date.

Thinking this just might be the best Christmas ever, she bubbled with good cheer and found herself wanting to tease a smile out of him. "Do I need to have my father's Santa suit dry-cleaned or will you be providing your own wardrobe for the evening?"

He snorted, his mouth creeping up at the corners as she'd hoped. "You worry about what you're going to wear, Li'l Miss Christmas Spirit. I'll take care of my suit."

"So long as it's not green with pointy toes, Mr. Grinchy."

He laughed. "Deal."

They stared at each other long moments, so long Abby couldn't help but wonder what he was thinking, couldn't help but wonder what had prompted his invitation. Was it possible that she wasn't the only one with visions of more than sugar plums dancing through her dreams? Could he at this very moment want to whisk her off her feet and carry her back to her bed and have a repeat? Why bother going to the bedroom? Kitchens were always good for cooking up something hot.

He cleared his throat, coughed, shook his head a little. "See you tomorrow night at the hospital. Thanks again for the fudge."

With that, he took his goodies and left.

Abby wrapped her arms around her apron-covered waist and danced around the kitchen while singing along with one of her favorite Christmas tunes.

She was going to the hospital Christmas party with the most amazing, sexy, wonderful man she'd ever met.

God, she loved Christmastime and if she wasn't careful, she just might end up loving Dirk, too.

"Bay one has a probable UTI," Abby told Dirk when he stepped out of the exam area where he'd just been seeing a patient in. "White blood cell count is twelve thousand, with neutrophils slightly elevated. There's a trace of blood and plus four bacteria in the urine. The patient reports tenderness in the abdomen and in the mid-low back."

Dirk nodded, without glancing directly at her.

Abby sighed. He'd seemed a bit distant tonight. She'd been dreaming of dashing through the snow like lovers with him ever since he'd issued his invitation to the Christmas party. Okay, before then. Way before then. She'd been dreaming of Dirk since the morning they'd ended up in bed together. Hadn't she known not to get her hopes up after the way he'd *dashed* out of her house after they'd made love? But she just couldn't seem to help herself where Dirk was concerned.

Reminding herself that she was a registered nurse, a professional, and on the job, she followed Dirk into the bay, telling herself to keep her mind—and eyes!—off the man in front of her, even if he did look fab-u-lous in his hospital-issue scrubs.

Obviously, he didn't spend his days inside, baking. Not with the taut definition in his upper arms, the strength in his neck and shoulders, the taper of his waist, the… Abby gulped. *Focus! He is not a Christmas package waiting for you to unwrap him. He's a highly respected emergency physician.*

But she'd really like to unwrap Dirk.

Focus! Focus! Focus!

"Hello, Mrs. Youngblood," he greeted the thin lady with streaky brown-blond hair and pinched facial features. "The nurse was just telling me about your lab results. It appears you have a serious urinary-tract infection. Tell me what's been going on."

Dirk examined the patient while the lady told him of her symptoms, when they'd started and how they'd gotten much worse during the night to the point she'd decided she couldn't wait until morning to check in with her primary care provider.

"No history of kidney stones?"

Mrs. Youngblood shook her head, her expression easing very little. "My husband has them, but I never have. Are they contagious?"

"No. You can't catch kidney stones from another person." Dirk pressed on her thin abdomen, attempting to palpate organs. "Any vaginal symptoms?"

"I don't think so," she denied, her hand guarding her belly as Dirk examined her. "It just really burns when I urinate. And feels like my bladder is going to turn inside out when I go, too."

"Have the medications given since you've arrived helped?"

"Yes." Although you sure couldn't tell it by the woman's grimace. "When I first got here I was miserable. The pain hasn't completely eased, but I'm a lot better."

Dirk washed his hands then turned to his patient. "I'm going to write a prescription for some antibiotics. You'll need to follow up with your primary care provider within the next couple of days." He began writing out orders. "Do you need a note for work?"

The woman shook her head. "I work from home as a medical billing clerk."

"Great." Dirk turned to Abby, meeting her eyes for the first time since they'd entered the room, and he smiled.

A real smile that reached those gorgeous blue eyes and pierced right into her heart.

Relief flooded Abby. Did he have any idea as to the lethalness of his smile? Probably. She soaked up every drop of his potency, letting the intensity of her emotions flow through her veins.

"Mrs. Youngblood," he said, his gaze flicking back to his patient. "The nurse will get you ready for discharge. If you have any additional problems or get worse before morning, I'd suggest you return to the emergency department for a recheck."

An hour later, the emergency department was in full swing. Every bay was full. Both physicians and the nurse practitioner on duty were at full stretch.

Abby adjusted a breathing mask over an asthma patient's mouth and nose, preparing to administer a beta-agonist medication via a nebulizer to rapidly open up the restricted airways.

"You may feel a little shaky and jittery after the medication starts working," she warned her patient. "The process that causes the bronchial tubes to dilate also speeds up the heart rate. Don't let the reaction alarm you as that's a natural and expected response to the medicine."

She turned on the nebulizer and waited to

make sure the patient's wheezing slowed before she stepped out of the bay to check on her next patient.

Dirk was with him—a morbidly obese man who'd woken up with a sharp tightness in his chest that took his breath. They'd started him on meds immediately on arrival, done tests, including an EKG that showed left ventricular hypertrophy and a possible blockage. They'd stabilized him while awaiting the results of his cardiac enzyme tests.

"I read your chest X-ray, Mr. Lytle. Your heart is enlarged, showing signs of your high blood pressure and congestive heart failure, but that shouldn't have caused you to wake up with chest pain. I don't see anything acute on the films, but your troponin level is slightly elevated. That's a myocardial muscle isoenzyme that elevates when the heart isn't getting enough oxygen. I'm going to admit you to the cardiac-care unit for close observation. The cardiologist on call has been notified you're here and will be by soon. He'll schedule you for a cardiac catheterization, likely for in the morning. That way, if there are any blockages, he can repair them immediately."

Abby began to prepare to have the patient transferred to the cardiac-care unit while Dirk answered the questions of the patient and his wife.

The rest of the night passed quickly. The E.R. was still bustling come shift change. An hour past time for her to have left, Abby clocked out, exhausted and feeling a little woozy.

Dirk had still been with an abdominal pain patient who'd come in minutes before shift change. Abby had offered to stay, but the day-shift nurse had taken over and had things under control.

She'd felt relieved at the reprieve, and surprised at how tired she was. The night had been busy, but no more so than dozens of others she'd worked, but she just wanted to go home, crawl into bed and pass out.

She rarely got sick, but definitely her stomach churned at the thought of breakfast. Maybe she'd just skip her usual light meal before going to bed.

Hopefully, she'd feel better once she got some sleep.

She hoped she wasn't coming down with something, especially so close to Christmas.

Regardless, no way would she let a little nausea and fatigue get her down when she had a date with Dirk for the Christmas party on Saturday evening.

CHAPTER FOUR

"DON'T tell me you unwrapped a Christmas present early and found Dr. Kelley inside, because if that's the case, I'm changing what I put on my wish list for this year." Medical floor nurse Danielle Booker draped her arm around Abby's shoulder on Saturday night at the hospital Christmas party being held in the ballroom of a nearby hotel.

Abby glanced away from where she watched Dirk talk with a couple of other physicians. When the conversation had turned to golf, she'd excused herself. She'd needed a few moments to breathe. Dirk had been the perfect attentive date, but the tension between them was so palpable it threatened to cut off her windpipe. Between that and his obvious discomfort at being at the party, Abby was wound tighter than a spool of ribbon.

"I'm waiting." Danielle tapped her slinky black high heels against the ballroom floor. "Were you such a good girl this year that Santa arranged for Dr. Kelley to be in your stocking?"

"Now isn't the time for details about my relationship with Dirk." Not to mention that she didn't know how to define their relationship.

"You're admitting you have a relationship with *Dirk*?" Her friend put emphasis on the use of his given name rather than his title of Dr. Kelley.

He'd been Dirk from the moment she'd glanced into his eyes and felt as if she were drowning in a blue sea of Christmas ribbon. With all her volunteering with the community outreach program, she hadn't found the time to call her best friend and they'd been on different shifts at the hospital. She hadn't told anyone about the morning she'd spent with Dirk. Perhaps if their relationship hadn't ended almost as fast as they'd started… And if they'd ended, what was tonight about? And why did she fluctuate between giddy and the need to protect her heart?

"I'm not admitting anything. Not here." Abby's gaze shifted to him again. Just looking at him made her feel as if she was all tangled up and would never be able to free herself. "But I like him, if that's what you're asking."

"You like him? Girl, that isn't 'like' I see in your eyes," Danielle teased, her grin growing bigger in direct proportion to Abby's face growing hotter. "You are so telling me everything soon."

"Everything," Abby agreed. Which was what? Dirk hadn't called or even talked to her at the hospital other than about patients and to confirm what time to pick her up. After his Santa debut and him asking her out for tonight, she'd jumped every time her phone had rung, hoping he'd call. She'd been disappointed every time. Disappointed that he hadn't made any effort to talk to her outside the parameters of work.

Until tonight.

Tonight, he'd been a considerate date, if quiet,

taking her white faux-fur wrap and gloves to the designated coat room, ensuring she had everything she wanted to drink and eat, even making the comment that her goodies tasted better than the ones supplied by the party's caterer.

Yet that ever-present awkwardness, awareness, kept her slightly on edge, not letting her completely relax, making her stomach stay slightly knotted with tension. That's why she'd needed a breather. Being so close to Dirk, his hand occasionally resting possessively on her back, she'd been on the verge of swooning from lack of air.

On the verge of grabbing his hand and dragging him to a room and kissing him like crazy in hopes of abating whatever this burn inside her was.

Abby covered her mouth with her hand, biting back a slight smile at what Dirk would do, say, if she marched over to him and did just that. Bet that wouldn't do a thing to ease the edginess she'd sensed about him all evening. Because of her? Or the Christmas party?

Danielle eyed her a moment, taking note of exactly what Abby wasn't sure, just that her friend's smile faded. "You okay? You look flushed."

Any flush on her face was from her thoughts, not from not feeling okay. Actually, the bug that had been bothering her earlier in the week was sticking around. But, fortunately, by the time Dirk had arrived she'd been fine. When he'd looked at her as if she was more mouth-watering than any piece of peppermint candy, had told her she was beautiful, well, she'd been over the moon.

If she'd stop trying to label whatever was happening between them and could just enjoy the fact that something was happening, everything would be wonderful.

She visually sought out where he still stood with the group of golfing physicians. He wasn't saying much, just listening to the others. Dirk didn't have to say much. The man would stand out in any crowd. Not just because of his height or his good looks or even his quick intelligence. No, he'd stand out because of the confident way he held himself, the pure aura of testosterone that clung to him and demanded women take notice, even though he seemed oblivious to the fact he was gorgeous.

Abby noticed. From his thick black hair to the tailored lines of his dinner jacket and trousers to the pointed toes of his Italian shoes, she noticed. And liked. She definitely liked.

"How could I not be okay?" she practically sighed, wondering if Danielle would scoop her up if she melted into an Abby puddle. Dirk liquefied her insides. Any moment she might slosh to the floor.

"Right," Danielle replied, her gaze following Abby's. "Got to admit, that man is fine. A little quiet and brooding for my taste, but he is easy on the eye."

Very easy on the eye. She'd seen more than one envious look her way when they entered the hotel ballroom.

"Just because he doesn't like Christmas doesn't mean he's brooding," Abby defended. "Plus, he isn't quiet once you get to know him. He has a great sense of humor."

Just recalling how he'd teased her made her insides toasty warm.

"I didn't know Dr. Dreamboat doesn't like Christmas and I still think he's brooding," Danielle pointed out.

Okay, so maybe a little brooding.

"The man keeps to himself, doesn't socialize, rarely talks to anyone outside anything to do with a patient or work. That's okay, mind you. He's probably just a private person, but that's not my style. Although…" she glanced toward where Dirk stood "…in his case, I could be convinced to make an exception." Danielle gave a little shake of her head. "Seriously, he doesn't like Christmas? Talk about your opposites attracting. Does he know you're the Queen of Holiday Cheer?"

"He knows." Recalling their conversation about the holidays, Abby tried not to wince. She'd just focus on the positive. "He likes my peanut-butter fudge."

"I'll just bet he does." Danielle snickered.

Abby rolled her eyes, but couldn't keep her smile from her face. "He stepped in and played Santa the other day at the community center, too."

See, there was another positive. Dirk had been there when she'd needed him. How many people could she say that of throughout her life so far?

"You're kidding! Dr. Kelley was Santa?" Danielle's mouth dropped open. "Now I know I'm changing my Christmas wish list. You should have told me. I could have come and sat in his lap."

Um, no. If any grown-up had been going to sit in Dirk's lap, Abby had dibs.

"My Santa canceled very last minute and I couldn't find a replacement. He saved me from canceling the event. Plus, he did a good job." Abby laughed at her friend's amazed expression. "Seriously, he did."

Mostly. He hadn't seemed to enjoy himself, but he had stayed until every kid in line had gotten their time with Santa. Not every busy doctor would have given up so much of his free time.

Okay, so he professed not to like Christmas. He was here at the Christmas party. He'd played Santa. Next thing you knew she'd have him out caroling or ringing bells for charity donations. Hey, it could happen. She was here with him, wasn't she? He was taking her home, wasn't he?

As if sensing her gaze, Dirk looked up. Laser-blue fire flew from across the room, flooding her belly with the sensation of a curly Christmas ribbon having been stretched out and released.

Wow, but the man packed a wallop.

First saying something to the men he stood with, he headed toward her. Tall, handsome in his dark suit, his eyes solely trained on her, as if she were the only person in the room, the only person who mattered. His hand touched her elbow and her world shifted off its axis.

"Hi, Dr. Kelley. Great party, huh?" Danielle smiled at Dirk, taking a sip of her wine.

"I suppose." Dirk's gaze briefly touched on

Danielle, but immediately returned to Abby. His eyes had the same look in them that he'd had at the "Pictures with Santa," a *rescue me, please* one. He held her gaze, his thumb stroking over her bare arm. Did he realize he was doing that? Would he please stop? The more he touched, the more she wanted him to touch. Not good. Her bosses were all here!

When she went to pull away, his hand enveloped hers, clasping her fingers in his slightly clammy ones.

Oblivious to Dirk's discomfort, Danielle sent Abby an impressed look, smiled widely, then excused herself under the pretense of getting another glass of wine.

"I'm not going to be able to stay much longer, Abby."

She nodded as if she understood, but she wasn't exactly clear. Had he gotten a call from the hospital? Due to the party, they were operating on a skeleton staff. Both Dirk and Abby were on call, so it was a possibility. Although she couldn't imagine why that would make him nervous.

"I'm sorry."

"What are you sorry for?"

"Not wanting to stay at the party you planned."

Work hadn't called. He just didn't want to be there. Abby bit the inside of her cheek, studying him.

As his gaze skimmed over the Christmas decorations Abby had thought gave just the right touch, he winced. "If it were any other kind of party…"

Than Christmas. He didn't have to say the words.

There was something about the way his eyes darkened, the way his body tensed, that had her squeezing his hand. She didn't want to leave, but neither did she like the tortured expression in his eyes. "It's okay. We can go whenever you like. Most of the good stuff has already taken place."

"Good stuff?" He focused on her face as if using her as a focal point to stay grounded.

"When the administrators acknowledged all the hard work everyone does every day of the year, when they acknowledged what a great staff we have, and, of course, when they gave away the gifts donated by local businesses."

His expression not changing, he studied her. "Sorry you didn't win."

"That's okay." She smiled up at him, feeling petite despite her four-inch heels.

"You look like a winner." His gaze raked over her Santa Claus red dress, pausing at where the waist dipped in before flaring out just above the knees.

"Thank you." She'd seen the dress, added the white wrap and the heels that were much more daring than anything she usually wore but couldn't resist, and known she had the perfect Christmas party ensemble.

She'd even splurged on new underwear. Not the granny whites like she usually wore. No, the tiny silk and lace garments beneath her dress kept up her Christmas red theme and made her feel less like that broken-down old toy and more like the shiny new one waiting to be played with under the Christmas tree.

Just in case.

As crazy as it was, she definitely wanted to relive all the things she and Dirk had done together, all the ways he'd touched her, kissed her, loved her body. She sighed in remembrance of the ways his hands and mouth had given her pleasure. So, so much pleasure.

"What are you thinking about?"

She glanced up, curious at the slight rasp to his voice. When her gaze collided with his, heat flushed her cheeks. She might not be able to read his mind, but he'd certainly read hers. He knew.

Knew exactly what she'd been thinking. Remembering.

It turned him on. Maybe as much as she was turned on. Could that be possible? Could he really feel the same?

"Earlier, when you asked, I promised to dance before the evening ended." His gaze never shifted from hers. "With you by my side, staying doesn't feel quite so impossible. Dance with me, Abby, then we'll go."

He was really going to dance with her? She'd already resigned herself that unless she danced with someone else, she wouldn't be making her way onto the dance floor.

Smiling, she let him lead her out. He took her into his arms and they swayed to the music in gentle rhythm.

"You're a good dancer." She'd imagined he hadn't wanted to dance because perhaps he couldn't. She should have known better about that, too. Dirk Kelley was a man of many talents.

"You sound surprised." He almost smiled. "It's been a while," he admitted, endearing himself even further, "but I guess it's like riding a bicycle. One of those things you don't really forget how to do."

"Why has it been a while since you've danced?"

Instantly, his arms stiffened.

"I just don't dance any more," he finally said.

Which wasn't really much of an answer and left her with a dozen questions he obviously wouldn't answer. Resisting a sigh, Abby laid her cheek against his chest, soaking in the warmth of being in his arms.

They danced, slow and in sync, their bodies touching, brushing against each other, his body heat melting her like a marshmallow in hot chocolate. Dirk made no motion to leave when one song turned into another.

"You smell good." He nuzzled her lightly, brushing his cheek against her hair. "Like fresh berries and cinnamon."

"You smell good, too," she admitted, amazed at her vocal cords' ability to make coherent sounds when her entire insides shook like she'd been trampled by stampeding reindeer.

"Are you having a good time?"

Nodding, she laid her cheek against his shoulder. From the corner of her eye, she saw Danielle give a thumbs-up and a suggestive eyebrow waggle and shake of her hips. She also noticed several of their colleagues watching them. Some with curiosity. Some with smiles.

A low, nervous chuckle rose up her throat.

"What?" he asked in a low voice, near her ear.

"Everyone thinks we're a couple."

His feet stilled a moment, as if he'd forgotten where they were, but his hands stayed at her waist. "I don't do couples, Abby."

She raised her head, stared at him. "Okay, we're not a couple." She took a deep breath. "What are we?"

He hesitated, looking torn. "I'm not sure."

Not the answer she'd hoped to hear. Then again, what had she expected? Feed the man a little fudge and he wouldn't be able to get enough of her?

She couldn't deal with his hot-cold attitude. Not and keep her sanity intact. Her heart intact.

"Then maybe you should get sure before we go any further, Dirk." Her heart banged against her rib cage in protest of her words. She wanted to go further. Lots further. But she wasn't a fool and wouldn't pretend to be one, not even for more time with Dirk. Regardless of how she felt, she deserved better than to be at his beck and call, available for comfort sex and Christmas parties. "I like you. A lot. But I don't want to end up with a broken heart and if you're not in this with me, then…" She shrugged. "Well, whatever this is needs to end now."

He studied her, his fingers splayed against her back, stroking over the material of her dress, possessively, distractingly. "I'd never hurt you, Abby."

"Not intentionally." Why were tears pricking her eyes? Why did she feel as if he was going to tell her goodbye? Why did that hurt so much? Technically, tonight was their first date. She would not cry. "But if I'm not careful where you're concerned, I will end up hurt."

Her heart protested it was way too late to start thinking about heart protection. She was crazy about Dirk. Way too crazy to walk away unscathed. Hadn't she fought tears more than once that he'd immediately had regrets about making love to her?

"You're right." He took a deep breath and she expected him to let her go, to push her away.

Instead, his hands tightened at her waist, as if he wasn't willing to let go, as if he clung to her for support. "I shouldn't have asked you here tonight."

"Why did you?"

"I didn't want to be here alone."

Had he only asked because she was convenient? Because he'd known she'd say yes? She bit the inside of her lower lip to hold it steady. He'd not made any grand promises. All he'd done was ask her to attend a Christmas party with him. She'd been the one to attach all sorts of sentimental meaning to his invitation.

Just as she'd attached all sorts of sentimental meaning to their morning together. Lord, she was a fool.

"But mostly because I can't quit thinking about you."

A soft moan escaped. That was more along the lines of what she wanted to hear. More along the lines of how she felt about him. Her breath caught, knotting in her throat.

"About making love to you." He shifted against

her, holding her more closely, pressing the length of her body to his. "I want you, Abby. I haven't stopped wanting you. Seeing you tonight, like this…" his gaze moved over the curve of her neck, her upswept hair "…touching you, I can't help but want to make love to you even though I know I shouldn't and you certainly shouldn't let me. Because regardless of how much I want you, I was serious when I said I don't do relationships."

"Why not?" She swallowed the knot, wondering at the raw emotions in his eyes. Emotions she wasn't positive had only to do with her, emotions he'd rarely bared, if ever.

He shook his head. "Not everyone wants the cozy Christmas fantasy of being part of a couple, Abby. That's not what I want."

The pain in his voice overshadowed his words, words she was sure were chosen to alienate her emotionally, revealed so much more than what he said. Did he realize how much he'd just exposed to her? That he'd given her a glimpse inside him?

A glimpse that undid any resolve she might have had to walk away.

"What do you want?" She held his gaze, clinging to his shoulders to remain steady on her feet as she prepared to expose her heart. "Because I'm not asking for some cozy Christmas fantasy. I just want you. So much I forget to breathe when I look at you."

He inhaled sharply, closed his eyes.

"Oh, Abs," he whispered against her forehead, sounding tortured and pleased all in the same breath. His jaw flexed. His eyes darkened then closed again. When they opened, possession shone. Possession and something so primal and needy that desire swept through Abby. His eyes asked questions much more potent than any he could speak.

She toyed with the soft hair at his nape, twirling the silky black strands around her finger, wondering if it was bad that she felt just as wrapped around his finger. "Will you take me home now, Dirk?"

He placed his thumb beneath her chin, lifted

her face. "I want to leave this monstrosity more than I can say, but are you sure?"

Concern flickered that he was calling what she'd thought a lovely Christmas party a monstrosity, but hormones ruled. That possessive look had her glutes tightening.

"Yes." She was sure she wanted to give him…everything. More. Needed to give him everything and more.

What the hell was he doing? Dirk wondered for the hundredth time that week.

Little Miss Merry Christmas was getting to him. And not just a little.

He'd been right when he'd told Abby she was beautiful earlier. She was. Absolutely stunning in her party dress.

But not as stunning as she'd been in nothing at all.

Dirk had been focusing on Abby to get through the party, had hung around the golf conversation just because it had been one of the few conversations going that had had nothing to do with the holidays.

Now, if he wanted to get out of the party without embarrassing himself, he had to keep his mind off Abby, off *that particular morning*, off how he'd lost himself in her body, how he'd felt whole inside for the first time in years. Even now, with her smiling up at him, he could lose himself in everything she was and almost forget the ever-present ache inside him at this time of year.

Her big hazel eyes were striking even without make-up accentuating them. Tonight they looked huge, like luminous stars guiding him to her. Her silky brown hair had been pulled up, but rather than the tighter style she wore for work, lots of strands hung loose, curling in loose tendrils. She wore a bright red dress that demanded attention and had captivated his from the moment she'd opened her front door, smiling at him as if he really was Santa come to fulfill her heart's every desire.

And those shoes.

He didn't know how she walked in the spindly red heels, how any woman walked in heels, but he appreciated how they pumped out Abby's calves, accented the toned lines of her legs. How they made his gaze want to keep traveling up those long lines, to unveil where they met, where he wanted to be. Oh, Abby.

Since his wife's death, he hadn't been a saint. He'd tried to ease the ache inside of him, only to realize he wasn't dating material any more.

But he'd never been as attracted to anyone as he was to Abby.

He knew better than to get involved, knew there could never be a relationship between them. Not one that would go anywhere. He'd suck the goodness right out of her life, weigh her down with his heavy heart. She was right to question him. Given the chance, he would break her heart.

Yet, he'd slept with her, figuratively and literally, after the first night they'd worked together. Sure, he'd backed off after that morning, but only because of how she'd looked at him with hope of a happy-ever-after. That look had had sweat prickling his skin and his heart fluttering in a panicked rhythm. Otherwise he'd have been burning up her sheets for the past two months.

He'd gotten out of her house stat and promised himself he'd keep his distance. So why had he agreed to be her Santa? Why had he asked her to come to this party with him? Sure, the administrator had questioned why he hadn't been going, but the guy would have gotten over it if he hadn't attended.

"Dirk?" Abby prompted when he failed to respond to her gutsy invitation to take her home.

He stared down into her blue-green eyes with their golden flecks, his hands around her waist, holding her to him while Christmas music played around them.

She was sweet and wonderful and giving. The more time he spent with her, the more he craved, the more he knew he should stay away. She believed in goodness and in the magic of Christmas. She gave of herself without asking for anything in return. Hadn't he just told her he didn't do relationships? Yet here she was, willing to give what he wanted. The truth was, he didn't want to go home alone, didn't want to face the demons of being at this party, just being alive during the holiday season, dredged up from his past, not when being with Abby made him feel better, less alone. She made him forget everything but her.

Just as on the morning they'd fallen into bed together, words weren't needed.

He was going to take all she'd give, knowing he had nothing to give in return and never would.

Bah, humbug. He really was a Scrooge.

CHAPTER FIVE

STANDING on her front porch, Abby fumbled twice before inserting the key into her door lock. Her hands shook like crazy.

She was crazy.

Hadn't Dirk told her he didn't do relationships? So why had they rushed from the Christmas party like teenagers? She laughed nervously. God, she felt like a teen on her way to a heated make-out session.

"Let me," he interrupted when, although she'd gotten the key into the lock, the release hadn't caught properly.

The lock clicked and Abby pushed the door open, practically falling into her foyer and dragging Dirk with her. He pushed the door closed with a resounding snap. The sound echoed through the darkness broken only by her

Christmas lights, which cast a magical aura over the foyer and living room thanks to the timers she kept them on.

"Come here," he growled, pulling her to him, taking her mouth by storm as he worked off her wrap, letting the heavy faux fur fall to the floor.

Yes, Abby thought, this was exactly how she remembered Dirk kissing her. As if she tasted sweeter than Christmas cookies and he was eager to go on a sugar binge.

He tasted just as sweet. Sweeter. His lips were marauding her mouth, his tongue tangling with hers as his hands slid over her body, touching, caressing, *claiming*.

Abby set about staking some claims of her own. Meeting him kiss for kiss, tangle for tangle. Tactically committing the hard lines of his body to memory, committing everything about him to memory.

"I want you so much."

She'd noticed. Oh, how she'd noticed!

"I want to savor every touch, every sigh that

escapes from your lips." He nibbled at her throat, at the base of her neck. Hot kisses that scorched her skin, bringing her blood to a boil.

His fingers searched out her zipper, slowly parted the back of her dress as his tongue traced over her carotid pulse, licking at the raging beat on her throat.

When his hand rested on her lower back where the zip ended, he turned his attention to the thin red straps holding up her dress.

Eyes locked with hers in the flickering colors of the Christmas lights, he looped one finger beneath the thin satin and slid the string off her shoulder, letting it dangle against her deltoid. He kissed where the strap had been. A soft, gentle, stomach-knotting kiss that shot an arrow of pleasure straight to the apex of her being. He turned to the other side and repeated the seductive gesture, his lips lingering on her bare shoulder.

"You are so beautiful, Abby. So sweet and perfect."

"I'm not perfect." Surely he knew she wasn't without her having to tell him. Surely he was just spouting lines. Although why he would when he already had her, she couldn't fathom. And, oh, how he had her!

He trailed more kisses over her shoulders, light, reverent. "You're the closest thing this side of heaven."

Dear Saint Nicholas alive! Did he have any idea what his praise was doing? What his kisses were doing?

Apparently, because he shimmied her dress over her hips to puddle in the floor around her feet.

She stood in her foyer, dressed only in the new red underwear she'd bought to match her dress and her high heels. If not for the blaze in Dirk's eyes, she might be cold, might be embarrassed. She was neither.

His gaze burned with desire. Deep, hot desire that told her everything. More. Desire that made her warm from the inside out. Hot.

She took his hand in hers. His eyebrow rose in question when she led him into the living room, rather than toward her bedroom. But she didn't explain herself, sensing that words would ruin the magical atmosphere. Instead, she took the throw blanket off the back of her sofa and tossed it into the floor in front of her fireplace, turned the knob that lit her gas logs, and met his gaze.

Swallowing audibly, he nodded, lay down with her on the blanket, pushing her back and staring down at her in the firelight. Wordlessly, his lips brushed her temples, her cheeks, her eyes, her throat. Slowly, his mouth worked over her skin.

She shifted, grasping at the buttons of his shirt, fumbling to undo them. She ran her hands inside the parted material of his crisp white shirt, loving the feel of his smooth chest against her fingertips, loving the rapid pounding of his heart beneath her palm.

She'd done that to him, made his heart beat wildly.

Like a snowman caught in a hothouse, Abby melted.

* * *

Dirk groaned, and gave up whatever hope he had of going slowly. He'd wanted to kiss every inch of her, to take things slowly, to do things right, instead of the desperate coupling they'd had last time. *Twice.* But where Abby was concerned he obviously could only go one speed. Head-on.

He shucked out of his shirt, groaned again at the feel of her hands rubbing over skin, over his shoulders, down his back. The pleasure Abby found in his body thrilled him, had him aching for more. She craned her neck to kiss his throat, his shoulders, his chest. Frantic, quick kisses that seared his flesh.

"So beautiful," he repeated, breathing in the spicy scent of her skin.

"If anyone in this room is beautiful, it's you," she whispered, pressing a kiss to his clavicle and reaching for his belt at the same time. "Hurry, Dirk."

If he hurried, everything would be over. Fast. She was driving him crazy. Each and every cell in his body had caught fire and burned with need.

Letting her pull his belt free, Dirk slid over her, pinning her beneath him, loving how she wrapped her arms around him, clinging to him.

"Hurry," she urged. "I need you."

Dirk kissed her until he thought he might explode, until their hands locked on to each other's rather than continue the frenzied exploration of each other's bodies.

"I need you, too, Abby." More than he'd ever imagined possible. Rolling slightly to his side, he reached for his waistband, planning to strip off his pants.

That's when he heard the sound of cold reality.

His cellphone.

"Don't answer it," she moaned, taking over where he'd stopped undoing his zipper. Her fingers brushed against him, and he inhaled sharply.

He wanted to ignore the phone, but he wouldn't.

"I'm on call." How he wished he wasn't. "No

one would call me this late unless there was an emergency."

Abby's face paled in the glow of the firelight. "Oh, God. I forgot."

He understood all too well. She made him forget, too.

Going into the foyer, he grabbed his jacket from the floor and removed his phone from the inside pocket. He listened to the caller for about thirty seconds then raked his fingers through his hair. "No problem. I'll be right there."

He hung up the phone and met Abby's soft, concerned gaze. She'd followed him into the foyer, stood next to him, her arms crossed protectively over her gorgeous body.

"It's okay. I understand," she said before he spoke. "My phone will likely ring at any moment."

"Probably." He went back to the living room, got his shirt, buttoned it with a lot less enthusiasm than he'd removed it, although with just as much haste. "There's been a gas leak in an apartment high-rise. One death. Dozens suffering inhalation injuries and respiratory distress. Patients are being diverted to several hospitals."

Stooping down and providing him with a delectable view of her backside that tempted him to say to hell with everything, Abby plucked up the blanket from the floor. She wrapped it round her shoulders, as if she didn't want him to see her almost naked body now that they'd been interrupted. "I'll get changed."

He started to speak, to tell her to get some rest while she could, that perhaps they'd already called in enough nurses without her. But her phone started ringing from inside her purse.

She gave a shaky laugh. "Wonder who that is?"

While she took the call, Dirk finished dressing, got his coat. A gentleman would wait until she finished her call, but he didn't. He left.

She already knew he wasn't a gentleman. Hell, he'd slept with her the day they met and had been about to take advantage of her yet again.

Still wanted to take advantage so badly

every cell in his body protested against the interruption.

She'd be wise to stay far, far away.

Perhaps that's why they'd been interrupted.

To give them both time to think about what they were doing. For Dirk to recall that Abby deserved better than what he'd give. For Abby to recall that she was young and beautiful and not bitter at the world, that she saw the goodness in life, the positive.

Things Dirk had quit doing long ago even if Abby had made him forget that for a short while.

Abby had put in eight hours of nonstop running from one patient to the next. Every bay had been full, with a rapid rate of turnover as patients were triaged into admission or treated and released.

The day shift would be arriving soon. Thank goodness. Her lower back ached and she felt more tired than she recalled feeling in a long, long time.

Surprised to find there wasn't another patient

waiting, she took advantage of the unexpected reprieve. Just a couple of minutes to disappear into the break room, lean against the wall and close her eyes, then she'd recheck the pneumonia patient in bay five.

"Things are starting to slow down. You should go home and get some rest. You look tired."

"Dirk." Abby's eyes shot open, surprised to see that he'd followed her. Not that she'd really expected otherwise, but he'd been the consummate professional all night. Not once had he let on that there was anything between them other than a doctor-nurse relationship, not once had he let on that had they not been interrupted they'd have made love most of the night.

Not once had he mentioned that when she'd come out of her bedroom, he'd left, breaking her heart into a thousand tiny shards that he'd left her without so much as a word.

"The others can handle the remainder of the shift." His tone was brusque, paternalistic. "Go home and get some rest, Abby. You look tired."

"I am tired, but I'll be fine until the end of shift." She would. Already, just looking at him, she could feel her energy level rising. Or maybe that was her hurt and anger coming to a head. "Are you coming back to my place?"

He sighed, raked his fingers through his dark hair, and glanced around the otherwise empty break room. "We need to talk."

Trying to read his expression, Abby searched his face. "I understand if you're too tired. It's just, well, I wanted you to know that if you want to come back, that's good by me. I could cook us something."

At least, she could cook him something. The thought of food made her stomach recoil. Or maybe it was the thought that he'd left her and she knew she wasn't going to like what he had to say.

His jaw worked back and forth. "I've been thinking about last night."

"Me, too," she admitted unsteadily. She couldn't quit thinking about last night, how they'd touched.

He grimaced. "Not like that, Abby. I've been thinking about what you said at the party about me needing to be sure before we went any further."

A feeling of impending doom crawled up her spine. Doom that made her stomach pitch so high it could have capsized a tanker.

"And?" she asked, not really wanting to hear his answer. Why was he backpedaling? She'd thought they'd come so far last night. Had everything only been physical? Was she really so naive as to have misread his looks, his touches so drastically?

"You were right to say that." He didn't meet her eyes, stared somewhere to her right at the wall. "If we continue on that path, I will hurt you and that's not what I want. I think we should just be friends."

"You're kidding, right?" She could tell by the look on his taut face that he wasn't. *Friends?* "If your phone hadn't rung, what we'd have been doing was a lot more than what just friends do," she pointed out, not willing to let him backtrack so easily.

"Which means we shouldn't have been doing what we were about to do. Fate stepped in."

Chin lifting, Abby's hands went to her hips. How could he be so dense? "Fate had nothing to do with that gas leak."

"But fate did rescue you from making a mistake, Abby. I have nothing to offer you beyond friendship. Nothing."

Did he really believe that? Looking at him, she realized he did, but not because he didn't want to offer her more, just that he didn't believe himself capable. What had happened to make him so cynical? To make him see the glass as half-empty? How could she look at him and see so plainly that he had so much more to give? So much more life in him than he saw in himself?

Why was it that when she looked at him she saw a world full of good and amazing things? A world full of Christmas every single day just because he was a part of her life?

She closed her eyes and counted to ten. "Okay,

if you want to just be friends, we'll just be friends."

She couldn't make him love her. Couldn't make him want to take a chance on loving her. She'd spent years living with her great-aunt, doing everything she could to earn the woman's love. In the end, she'd realized you can't make someone love you. Either they did or they didn't.

"I'm glad you understand." He let out a slow breath, looked relieved that she wasn't going to make a scene.

Had he expected her to stomp her feet and throw a fit? Wrong. But neither would she pretend everything was fine, when it wasn't.

"No." She shook her head. "I can't say that I understand, because I don't. Obviously I misread your feelings for me."

"Abs—"

"Don't," she interrupted, holding up her hand. "Don't say things you don't mean in the hope of making this easier. I like you, a lot. You obviously don't feel the same so, fine, end of story. We'll be friends."

So why didn't she believe he didn't feel the same? Why did she believe that something else had prompted him to back away? Something that ran so deeply through him he believed he had nothing to offer her but heartache? Something that had to do with his dislike of the holidays?

"You deserve better."

She nodded. "You're right. I do."

This time she was the one who left.

By the time she got home, she was throwing up. No doubt from the stress of the night and the sickening feeling that had crept in during their conversation.

Friends. He wanted to be friends. *Liar.* Who did he think he was kidding? He didn't look at her the way her *friends* looked at her.

Neither did she have sex with *friends.*

Or even almost have sex with her friends.

Really, she'd just like to know how it was possible for a man to look at her with fire in his eyes and ice on his tongue? Because his words had bit into her bitterly coldly. Frigidly. *Friends.*

Fine, if that's what he wanted, she'd be his friend.

She told herself all these things and more right up until that night, when she was scheduled to work with him.

Then she admitted the truth.

She couldn't be Dirk's friend. Not when she felt the way she did about him. If she didn't protect her heart, she'd end up wearing battle scars from their *friendship*. Scars that ran so deep she wouldn't ever recover.

No, she couldn't be his friend, but somehow she had to be his colleague, his nurse. She had to work with him and be the professional she was. Somehow.

Almost, she called in sick, but her illness had passed, had just been from a morning spent longing for what might have been. So she'd go to work and come face-to-face with a man who seemed determined to be *friendly*.

Seriously, it was enough to send her stomach into Churnville all over again.

CHAPTER SIX

DIRK hadn't slept much between ending his emergency call the morning following the Christmas party and reporting back in for a half-shift that evening. How could he when he couldn't stop thinking about Abby?

She'd agreed to his friend proposal, but he'd seen the hurt in her eyes. The confusion. She didn't understand.

Why had he let things get so out of control the evening before? Not that Abby had given him much choice. He'd looked into her eyes, heard the truth in her voice when she'd told him she wanted to make love, and he'd ignored all the reasons why they shouldn't.

Just as he'd ignored the reasons why he shouldn't have asked her to the Christmas party to begin with. Not that he'd meant to. The invitation had just slipped out of his mouth and she'd looked so happy when she'd said yes, he hadn't taken the words back.

Just as he hadn't taken them back when he'd agreed to be her Santa.

Seeing Abby happy did something to him, made him do things he ordinarily wouldn't do. Made him want things he shouldn't want.

When he had slept, he'd been haunted by treacherous nightmares. Had they been triggered by attending the Christmas party? Or just by the season he could never escape? Or from walking away from Abby when she was the best thing to enter his life in years?

Regardless, he'd welcomed the evening and the start of his abbreviated—due to the holiday party—shift. Right or wrong, he'd also welcomed seeing Abby again, welcomed everything about her, including the tray of goodies she'd left on the break-room table.

Mostly he just wanted to make sure she was okay. During the night, as they'd worked on patients, he'd felt her gaze on him, felt her studying him, trying to see beneath his surface. If she only knew what darkness lay beneath, in the depths of his soul, she'd have turned away, never wanting to look again.

If he wasn't careful, he was going to hurt Abby.

That and that alone should accomplish what he hadn't previously had the willpower to do.

He would ignore the attraction between them before he hurt her. Otherwise he'd end up taking every drop of sweetness from her and leaving her with nothing more than a barren tree with a few empty hangers where shiny ornaments had once glistened.

Abby deserved fullness of life, color and brightness, glittery packages, and tinsel, and twinkling lights. All the things he wasn't.

Having finished with the patient he had been tending, he stepped into the next bay, pausing in mid-step. Abby was cleaning the room, preparing for the next patient. She had to know he stood there, but she didn't look up to acknowledge him.

He turned to go, but the fact she ignored him irked.

She'd been polite all evening, courteous when discussing a patient. But other than regarding a patient, she hadn't spoken a word to him.

He didn't like it. They were friends, right?

"I saw you'd brought more goodies." He'd snagged a couple from the rapidly disappearing tray. "Those haystack things were great."

She nodded, not looking up from where she spread out a clean sheet. "I always bring lots of goodies this time of year. It's tradition."

She kept her tone even, but she was upset. She'd invited him to stay the day with her and he'd left her high and dry, told her he just wanted to be friends.

Idiot.

Dirk grabbed the corner of the sheet closest to where he stood and spread the material out, eliciting a surprised look from her. "You have a lot of Christmas traditions, don't you, Abby?"

"Yes." Taking a deep breath, she tucked the clean sheet in around the hospital bed. "Christmas traditions are important to me." She straightened, held his gaze then sighed. "Before you give me a lecture on all the woes of the holidays, let me just warn you that I'm a little cranky so you might not want to do that. Not tonight."

Dirk took a step back. Abby was cranky? Because of him. Because he'd refused to go with her. Because he'd said he just wanted to be friends.

"I'm sorry, Abby."

She snorted, rolling her eyes. "It's not that."

"Then what? Is Macy's all sold out of that gift you just have to buy still?" He tried to keep his tone light, to make a joke in the hope some of the usual sparkle would return to her eyes, but when he spoke of anything to do with Christmas a brittle edge always seemed to be present.

"Ha-ha. Too funny." Rather than sparkle, she rolled her eyes again. "For the record, I finished my shopping weeks ago."

She was probably one of those women who started next year's shopping the day after

Christmas. That seemed like the kind of thing Abby would do.

"If you must know," she continued, smoothing out an imaginary wrinkle on the expertly made bed, "I haven't felt well."

Her hand popped over her mouth as if she hadn't meant to say that out loud, as if she regretted that she had.

"What's wrong?" All desire to keep the conversation light vanishing, Dirk studied her. She didn't look ill. She looked…beautiful, almost ethereal, like the delicate angel on top of a Christmas tree.

"Don't look at me like that. I shouldn't have said anything," she huffed, but when he only stared, waiting for her to elaborate, she continued. "I'm fine. Really. Just a virus."

But she didn't meet his eyes and he placed his hand on her forehead.

"I don't have a temperature." She gave an exasperated sigh.

"Tell me what's going on. I'm a doctor, remember?" Again, he strove to keep his tone light, but her evasiveness worried him. The thought of her being sick worried him. "Maybe I can help."

He wanted to help. As a doctor to a patient, he told himself, even as he acknowledged his concern went beyond that of doctor-patient. As a friend to another friend, he corrected, but even that didn't cover the protective feelings the idea of Abby being ill spurred within him.

"Fine. I'll tell you, but just remember you asked for this." She picked at the pristine bedding, rubbing her fingernail over the white material. "I've been feeling tired. A little nauseated at times to where my appetite just isn't what it should be. I threw up this morning, but that's because I crie—" She paused again, flushing.

She must have spent as restless a day in bed as he had. Guilt hit him. He didn't want Abby to suffer because of him. He'd wanted to keep from hurting her, but he'd waited too late.

"You should have taken sick leave tonight."

"Why? Nursing staff are almost always short-handed as is." She frowned. "Besides, it's nothing much, really. I don't feel myself, but that's my own fault, isn't it?" Glancing up at him, her weak smile almost knocked him to his knees. "I do realize that I shouldn't have read so much into you asking me to the Christmas party, Dirk."

"I'm sorry I gave you the impression we could be more than friends." He wanted more than friendship. He wanted to be her lover. Without strings. Without having to worry about hurting her.

She lifted a shoulder in a mock shrug. "I should have known better."

"Why should you have known better, Abby? I was sending mixed signals." Saying one thing, wanting another. Why was he admitting this to her? Wasn't he only sending more mixed signals by doing so?

"Were you?" Her brow lifted. "I hadn't noticed."

The way she said it, so sarcastic, bugged Dirk. Abby was happy, bubbly even. Not today. Nothing about this conversation felt right. Sure, he'd expected tonight to be awkward, but they'd done awkward before. Had done awkward for two months with only a break when he'd agreed to be Santa. This went beyond that.

Something was wrong with Abby.

He thought of the long hours she worked, of all the volunteer work he knew she did. No doubt she was spending the time she should be sleeping baking Christmas candies.

"You're not getting enough rest."

She pushed an empty IV stand against the wall, out of the way. "I slept eight hours each of the past couple of days. I'm getting plenty of rest, Dr. Kelley."

His name came out with emphasis, coated with annoyance.

He followed her around the room. "Obviously your body needs more rest."

"Obviously," she agreed wryly, picking up a stray alcohol pad package from the counter. "But it's choosing the wrong time of year to tucker out on me. I've got too much to do to get sick right now."

"Like what? More spreading Christmas cheer stuff?"

Her eyes narrowed into an outright glare. "I like spreading Christmas cheer. If anything, volunteering makes me feel better about life. Not worse. Maybe you should try it sometime instead of all that bah-humbug stuff."

"Maybe when you're healthy, but at end of shift, you need to go home and get some sleep. Doctor's orders."

"This morning, after my shift ends, I'm picking up boxes of food to deliver to the poor." Her expression dared him to say anything. "After I finish that, I'm delivering fruit baskets to a nearby nursing home."

Boxes of food. Fruit baskets. Hadn't she mentioned something earlier in the week about volunteering in a soup kitchen, too? Plus, she'd been doing all this baking.

"Aren't you on schedule to work again tonight?" He knew she was. He knew each and every night they'd be working together. And the ones they wouldn't.

"I'm due here at seven. For the record, you're

not my doctor and I didn't ask for your advice, neither do I want it."

He crossed his arms, pinning her beneath his gaze. "So when are you planning to sleep?"

"After I get the fruit baskets delivered." She winced, confirming what he already suspected. She hadn't left much time for sleep. "Normally, I can do this and more without so much as blinking my eyes. Getting called in to work on the night of the Christmas party threw off my rhythm a little, that's all."

She didn't comment that he'd played a role in her rhythm being thrown off. She didn't have to. She had to be on the verge of exhaustion and whether she wanted his advice or not, she was going to get it.

"No wonder you're coming down with something," he scolded. "Didn't they teach you anything about taking care of yourself while you were in nursing school? Sleep is important."

Said he who had slept very little over the past few weeks. How could he when every time he closed his eyes his dreams took him back to the morning he'd made love to Abby? A morning where he'd felt guilty for taking advantage of her goodness. After that, he'd done all he could to avoid her, to keep things completely professional between them. Abby hadn't pushed, hadn't asked anything of him. Not until she'd asked him to play Santa.

He should have said no.

None of this would be happening if he'd just said no.

"I do this every year," she insisted, sounding more and more annoyed. "I just have a light virus or something. It's no big deal and really none of your business."

Dirk gritted his teeth, took a steadying breath, and managed to keep from pulling her into his arms to shake some sense into her.

"Yeah, well, you might try to kill yourself every year, but I've never been here to watch you run yourself ragged in the past," he reminded her, moving in front of her, placing his fingers on her chin and lifting her face so she had to look at him. "I'm going with you."

Her forehead wrinkled as her brows lifted high on her heart-shaped face. "Do what?" she scoffed, her hands going to her hips.

Yeah, that's pretty much what Dirk was wondering, too. *Do what?* But the thought of her pushing herself all day after working such long shifts back to back bothered him. Especially knowing she planned to come in and work another long shift despite the fact that she wouldn't be able to squeeze in more than a few hours' sleep at most.

None of his business? That bothered him, too. Right or wrong, he cared about Abby, didn't want her pushing herself so much. Friends could care about friends, could want to help each other.

"I'm going with you," he repeated, his tone brooking no argument. "You'll finish quicker and be able to get some of the rest you obviously need."

She regarded him a long moment, then her lips twisted into a rather sinister smile. "You're welcome to go with me, Dirk. Not because of me, but because you need a lesson in what Christmas is really about. Helping the needy is a great way to learn that lesson."

He didn't need to learn any such lesson.

"That's not why I'm going." He was going because she needed him, whether she was too stubborn to admit it or not. If easing Abby's self-imposed load counted as helping the needy, so be it.

"No, but it's definitely what you're going to learn. Come on, Scrooge. Let's finish our shifts so we can go make a difference in the world."

Abby snuck a glance at where Dirk helped pack more canned food and basic household supplies into a box that would later be given to a needy person.

She hadn't wanted him to come with her, didn't want him being nice to her, didn't want to be near him, period. How was she supposed to protect her heart when he insisted on helping her?

As much as she hated to admit it, he was right. She had overstretched herself, and appreciated his help so that she'd finish earlier. But there was so much to be done at this time of year. So much important work. Besides, sitting at home gave her too much time to contemplate that when she went home only Mistletoe cared. That she had no family to come home to, no family to share Christmas dinners, no family to sit around the tree with and open packages.

No one.

Her gaze lifted from the box she was packing, landing on the man across the table.

Why did looking at him bring how alone she was into focus so clearly? Why did looking at him make her see what she'd been able to hide from herself in the past? That, although she loved volunteering, she didn't do so selflessly. No, she also volunteered because doing so prevented her from thinking about how she'd spend another Christmas alone.

"You okay?"

Abby blinked at Dirk. Although he'd been terse when they'd first arrived, he had quickly impressed the other volunteers.

Volunteers who kept sending Abby sneaky

smiles and suggestive eyebrow wiggles. After her first few attempts at convincing her longtime friends that she and Dirk were only coworkers, friends, she'd given up. After all, she didn't buy the friends bit any more than they did. Besides, the more she'd protested, the bigger their smiles had grown.

"Abs? You okay?" he repeated.

She glanced at where Dirk had finished with his box and had lifted another to fill. A wave of dizziness hit her and she grasped hold of the table. What was wrong with her? To get sick right now would be so unfair.

"I'm fine," she lied, hoping she was imagining the sweat beads popping out on her forehead.

Maybe she should have said no for once, asked the ladies to get someone else. Anything so she didn't get ill in front of Dirk.

What was she thinking? Of course she couldn't have done that. Not when it would mean that someone's Christmas wouldn't be as special, as magical.

When it would mean going home and being alone.

She was fine. Or would be if Dirk would get back to packing and quit staring at her. It wasn't as if he knew she was struggling to keep up. She would not let him know just how much effort she was putting into this.

"Maybe you should rest for a few minutes," he suggested, boxing up more canned goods. "I'll finish this."

Or maybe she didn't have to tell him how much effort she was putting in. Maybe he already knew. Somehow. Probably that crazy connection they shared. The one he insisted on calling friendship.

She sighed.

"Or better yet…" He stopped what he was doing to pin her beneath his azure gaze. "Let me take you home where you can get proper sleep before you drop."

The two volunteers elbowed each other. Abby bit back another sigh, this one from fatigue, and straightened her shoulders. "There's no reason I can't finish, Dirk."

How dared he tell her what to do? Try to tell her what she needed? The only reason she'd agreed to let him come with her was because he needed a lesson in helping others, on what Christmas really meant. She should have said no. Him being here obviously stressed her.

"No reason except you need to rest."

She ignored his comment. Drawing on all her inner strength to hide just how woozy she felt, she smiled at the ladies watching them curiously. "Once we get these packed, we'll divvy them up and take the ones on my list to deliver. Dr. Kelley can go home and rest."

Eyeing her like a kid studied a sole, tiny package labeled for him under the Christmas tree, Dirk frowned. A tightly controlled muscle jumped at the corner of his mouth. "This is too much after working all night. Call and cancel the fruit basket delivery."

Tempting, but then who would deliver the baskets? Besides, she was pretty sure it was the stress of being near him making her feel so bad. That and the virus. If he'd just quit looking at her…

"No." She couldn't cancel her activities. Sure, she'd been a little out of sorts. That wasn't any reason to let down those depending on her. They needed her help to make their Christmas all it should be, all hers wouldn't be.

"Abby, if you're not feeling well, Joyce and I can finish this up," Judy, the lady in charge, offered, placing her hand on Abby's shoulder.

Dirk smiled smugly, obviously viewing the woman's offer as reinforcement that he was right, that she should do as he wanted. Enough was enough.

"Seriously." She made eye contact with the elderly lady she'd bonded with while still in nursing school on her first volunteer project. "I'm fine. I just made the mistake of mentioning to Dr. Overprotective—" she flicked her thumb toward Dirk, hoping how much he meant to her didn't show "—that I'd been feeling under the weather."

"Nothing serious, I hope," Judy said sympathetically, completely ignoring that Abby had said she was fine.

"Of course not. I've just had a little nausea and fatigue for a few days. No big deal." At the woman's look of concern, Abby added, "Nothing contagious."

At least, she didn't think so. If so, surely some of her coworkers would be having symptoms by now since she'd been fighting this for more than a week. For that matter, Dirk would be having symptoms. He'd definitely had up-close exposure the night of the Christmas party.

"I'm definitely not contagious," she repeated, hoping to reassure her friends.

Her face brightening, Joyce clapped her hands together gleefully. "Ooh, when you walked in today, I just knew there was something different about you. Beside the fact you brought this gorgeous man with you." The older woman sent a knowing smile Dirk's way then returned her attention to Abby. "Just look at how you're glowing."

"Glowing?" Abby's mouth dropped just as Dirk's can crashed to the concrete floor as the woman's meaning sank in. The sharp intake of his breath almost drowned out the loud clang. Abby was surprised the thunderous beat of her heart didn't deafen them all. "If you're implying… I think you're making a wrong assumption."

The two smiling volunteers looked at each other, then back at Abby and Dirk, their smiles fading as realization dawned. "You're not pregnant?"

"Uh, no." Abby coughed into her hand, trying to make sure she worded this correctly so she didn't end up as before, protesting to the point that she was only convincing her friends of the opposite. "Of course I'm not pregnant. I can't be."

Dirk had used a condom. Although she'd been wrapped up in what they'd been doing, she was sure he had used protection. She'd found two opened foil pouches.

She faked another cough, whether to show her symptoms were from something else entirely or just to buy a few more seconds to think of what to say she wasn't sure.

"You ladies are as bad as Dirk about overreacting." She laughed as if their suggestion was preposterous. It was preposterous. Pregnant. Her. No way. "I've just been pushing myself a little too hard with the holidays and have picked up a minor bug of some sort at work. You know how I'm exposed to everything in the emergency room. It's a wonder Dirk isn't sick, too."

But even as she gave the excuse she counted back the days since her last menstrual period and came up with a too-high number. Way too high a number. Oh. My.

This time she inhaled sharply, would have dropped a can if she'd been holding one. Her fingers curled into her palms, her nails digging painfully into the soft flesh.

Could she be? Was it possible? She'd never considered the possibility, hadn't dared to consider her lovemaking with Dirk might leave her pregnant. They were consenting adults who'd used a condom. Not overzealous teenagers who'd had unprepared-for sex.

She wasn't pregnant. Or was she?

She wanted kids. Someday, she wanted kids a lot. But not while unmarried and by a man who said he wanted to just be her friend. She wanted the dream. Snuggling in front of the fireplace together, sipping hot cocoa, enjoying each other's company. She'd take his hand and place it over her much, much thinner belly from where she'd finally stuck to that exercise routine and, with hope in his eyes, he'd ask if she was. She'd nod. They'd fall into each other's arms and be so happy together. A family. No more lonely Christmases. No more lonely ever.

But never had she imagined being pregnant, unwed and finding out while volunteering at a food bank with the prospective father having told her just the day before that they were only friends. By the look on Dirk's face, this obviously wasn't how he'd envisioned the moment, either.

Powerless to stop her hand, her palm settled

over her abdomen. Was Dirk's baby growing inside her? Would she give birth to a little boy or girl with eyes so blue they left the sky envious? With hair so inky black the night paled in comparison?

If so, what in the world would she do about an unplanned pregnancy by a man who she technically barely knew, but felt as if she knew better than anyone she'd ever met? A man who said he only wanted to be friends and professed not to even like Christmas?

CHAPTER SEVEN

DIRK'S ears roared with the intensity of a jet taking off inside his head. Any moment he expected the backdraft to knock him off his feet and send him crashing against the wall.

Mentally, he was already thrashing about the room. Emotionally, he'd already crashed and gone up in flames.

Abby's big hazel eyes had widened with shock, had darkened with unwanted possibilities, with fear, then softened as her hand pressed her lower abdomen.

Hell, no. She couldn't be. He'd used a condom both times they'd made love. He always used a condom. Always.

But, hell, how old had the condoms in his wallet been? Although he hadn't lived the life of a monk over the past four years, he hadn't exactly had a high prophylactic turnover rate, either. He'd never considered checking the condoms' expiration date. They'd been, what? About a year old, maybe? God, it was possible they'd expired.

He should have checked. He should have known better. He was a doctor, trained not to make the mistakes a seventeen-year-old boy would make.

Abby might be pregnant, and it was his fault.

He didn't want her to be pregnant.

The two women who'd hovered over them both like mother hens were obviously drawing the same conclusions.

Despite her protest, Abby might be having a baby. His baby. The slightly stunned expression on her pretty little face said so.

Another woman, another pregnancy, swept through his memories. Sandra excitedly telling her news. Lord, he'd been scared. After all, he'd still had a few years of residency left. But he'd looked into her eyes and he'd hidden his fear, had swept her into his arms and spun her around. A baby. Shelby. And now, would there be another baby?

Sharp pain zigzagged across his chest at the thought.

Both volunteers turned to him, expectation and protectiveness of Abby in their eyes. He couldn't blame them. He felt like beating the crap out of him, too, for doing this. He deserved worse if he'd made her pregnant.

Judy crossed her arms over her chest, her head bent slightly to one side, as if to say, *Well?*

Uh-huh. He wasn't going to have that conversation with two strangers watching, listening to every word.

Abby wasn't pregnant. And if she was… Hell, he didn't know what they'd do if she was.

Regardless, that was a private conversation. Not one for women he'd just met, even if they were longtime friends of Abby's and treated her like a favorite niece.

Following Abby's lead, Dirk drew on acting skills he'd honed in the days following Sandra and Shelby's deaths, days in which he'd been dead inside but had had to go on, puting on a front for the world. Had put on a show for his friends and family who'd not been able to look at him without pity in their eyes. Pity he'd tired of and left behind. In late spring he'd started searching for another position, knowing he couldn't face another holiday season under their watchful gazes. In June he'd accepted the position in Philadelphia, finished up his Oak Park contract, and had started in the emergency room in October.

And met Abby. Possibly impregnated her.

"This is the last of the boxes, Abby. You ready to pack them into my truck so we can go?" God, he hoped so, because he wanted away from the prying eyes. "We've still got to go pick up those fruit baskets and get them delivered. Unless I can convince you to cancel out so you can rest and properly get over this *virus*."

Did his voice sound normal? Or could everyone in the room hear his panic? See how his insides quavered at the thought he might have made Abby pregnant?

"I, uh…" Her hand fell away from her belly. She turned to him, her expression so tentative and vulnerable that something fragile deep in his chest cracked open and bled freely, gushing, leaving him weak. "Yes, I'm ready. Let's get these loaded."

Stunned by the rush of emotions, Dirk just stood, unable to move, unable to put on a show, only able to watch Abby smile briefly at the other volunteers and walk over to a far corner of the room. She had a dolly in her competent little hands within minutes.

"It's not much," she said, rolling the dolly toward him. "But it will do at a pinch."

He would have welcomed any excuse to get away from the mother hens' knowing looks. He hightailed it, boxes in tow, moving at record speed, leaving the three women alone.

Even before he'd made it out the door Judy's excited squeal echoed throughout the building, across the city, across his stampeding heart.

"Tell me the truth. You're pregnant, aren't you?"

He turned, waiting at the doorway to hear Abby's answer. The two women had practically pounced on her, were holding her hands and excitedly asking her questions.

As if sensing he still stood there, she glanced toward the doorway, met his gaze. Deep emotions shot across the room, deep pleas. Pleas for exactly what Dirk wasn't sure, neither was he sure he wanted to know.

Abby needed him. How could he be there for her when there wasn't anything left of him to give?

"Tell us." Judy wrapped her arm around Abby's shoulder in a motherly hug. "Are you pregnant or not?"

"Regardless, we love you and are here for you," Joyce added. "You know that."

Did they even know he still stood here? He held his breath, waiting, wondering, knowing it was impossible, knowing it was damned well possible. He'd made love to Abby quite vigorously. Twice.

"Don't be silly and start rumors," she said with

a falsely bright voice, looking from one of the ladies to the other, then at him. Their gazes met, clung to each other.

Don't say it, Abby. Don't say that there is any possibility you might be pregnant.

"Of course I'm not pregnant."

Which should have relieved him, but her eyes told a different story.

All eight of Santa's reindeer drop-kicked Dirk in the gut at once, knocking his breath out of him and stomping him to smithereens while he was down.

Abby might be pregnant with his baby.

What had he done?

"This is crazy," Abby protested when Dirk pulled his truck into a parking space at the pharmacy.

After his terse "We'll talk when we've finished delivering" they'd continued in virtual silence. They'd delivered to the public housing residents on her list. They'd smiled and said all the appropriate things to the grateful recipients, but there had definitely been underlying tension.

Abby didn't feel tense. Not really.

She felt numb. Perhaps in denial. Yes, she'd missed her period. Two of them. But she'd been irregular on occasion in the past, so that was the likely explanation. Certainly, she hadn't thought anything of her missed periods. They'd always come and gone as they pleased.

Plus, there were the increased demands on her time with her Christmas volunteering. Although she loved what she did, believed one hundred per-cent in making the holidays brighter for others, the workload was stressful.

Stress. Stress did a lot of things to the body and could be the reason for the missed periods. She hoped it was. Really hoped it was.

Which was why she didn't want to walk into the drugstore and buy the item she knew he'd come for, although, from the moment he'd turned off the ignition, they'd just sat in silence.

What if she was pregnant? What if the test came back positive? Then what? Hadn't he al-ready told her he didn't do relationships? Yet he'd gone with her today. God, the man confused her. She really couldn't be pregnant.

"I'm probably not." She battled the tightening of her throat that she might be. "You used condoms."

She was twenty-five years old. Why was her face on fire at saying the word "condom" out loud? Here they were discussing the possibility of having a baby and she was blushing over contraceptives?

Gripping the steering wheel, he stared out the windshield at some unknown object. "Women get pregnant all the time despite having used a condom."

God, he sounded so terse, so like he hoped she wasn't pregnant. Despite understanding and feeling exactly the same way, his reaction stung. No doubt having her pregnant with his child would be a nightmare to Dirk. After all, he'd only slept with her because they'd been grieving. Although, admittedly, the intensity of his grief had caught her off guard. But there had been sexual attraction between them, too. Lots of sexual attraction.

She hadn't imagined the sparks, the way his gaze had lingered when they'd first made eye contact, the way he'd seemed shocked by the physical awareness zipping back and forth. But women used for sex weren't supposed to end up pregnant.

Oh, God. Dirk had used her. Two months had passed before he'd asked her out again. That had only been after she'd initiated contact outside work, after getting him to be Santa. The physical attraction was there, but obviously Dirk wasn't interested in a relationship.

The morning they'd made love, they'd shared a physical attraction, an emotionally wrenching work experience, sex, a budding *friendship*, and, possibly, made a baby.

Just the thought had her hand going back over her belly. Was Dirk's baby nestled inside her, growing and wanting to be loved? If she was pregnant, and, God, she hoped she wasn't, but if she was, she would love this baby. A baby she and Dirk had made.

Maybe made.

"Don't do that," he snapped.

"What?" Startled by his outburst, she jerked around in the passenger seat to look at him.

His blanched white fingers clenched the steering wheel. His face looked just as pale. "Cover your abdomen as if…as if you are."

Was the idea that repugnant to him? Of course it was. She was the one longing for a family, longing for someone to love, and the idea of an unplanned pregnancy left her in a cold sweat. No wonder Dirk was pale. Such a gorgeous man probably had loads of people to love, loads of people who loved him. A baby with a woman he'd used was the last thing he'd want or need.

Then another thought hit her. Was there someone already in his life?

Oh, God. Was that why he was so upset? Although she'd never heard of anyone special in his life, she wasn't privy to the intimate details of his life. Actually, his private life was just that. Private. She'd never heard anyone speak of outside work activities involving the man gripping the steering wheel so tightly there was likely to be finger impressions when he let go.

"Is there someone in your life, Dirk? Someone who will be upset if I'm pregnant?"

He didn't answer her, just gripped the steering-wheel all the tighter, his fingers digging into the dark leather. "*If* you're pregnant. We need to know what we're dealing with."

A baby. That's what they were dealing with. She wanted to scream at him. But she bit her tongue, reined in her anger. She couldn't lash out. Not when deep down she didn't want a pregnancy any more than he did. It was just…just what? She wanted him to be happy he'd made her pregnant when she wasn't happy about the idea herself?

Wasn't that irrational? Could she blame it on hormones? She winced. She could, but she wouldn't believe it. But if she wasn't pregnant, this was all immaterial, all stress and angst for nothing.

She sighed. As much as she didn't want to walk into the store and purchase a pregnancy test, he was right. They had to know. Had to figure out what they were going to do if she had gotten pregnant *that* morning.

There went the rest of her life, all riding on the results of a plastic stick.

She reached for the door handle, but Dirk's hand shot out, stopping her.

"No, that's not fair to you. I'll go and buy the test." He squeezed her hand, held on another few seconds, as if for his own reassurance. "I'm sorry I snapped at you, Abby. This isn't easy. Just… just wait here."

With that, he leapt out of the truck and flew into the store as if he'd been snacking on Santa's reindeers' magic corn.

Dirk supposed it was only appropriate that he be surrounded by Christmas hell while he waited on Abby's sofa to find out if he'd made her pregnant.

That he should be reminded of how he'd taken off her red dress, lain on the floor in front of her fireplace the last time he'd been in her house.

Had that really only been two nights ago?

Everything had seemed so right. But it hadn't been. Later, when not driven by surging testosterone, he'd been glad his phone had interrupted them. Too bad his phone hadn't rung the morning they'd had sex.

Abby might be pregnant.

His brain kept telling him the test would be negative. But his heart, his heart had seen the very realistic possibility on her face.

He suspected Abby didn't need the test to know the results, whether she'd admit as much to herself or not.

Hearing the bathroom door, he glanced up, waiting for her to reappear, to tell him the bad news.

Carrying the slender plastic test, she sat on the sofa beside him and placed the test on the coffee table.

"Well?" he asked, unable to wait another minute without knowing and unable to decipher her expression.

Her cheeks pink, she shrugged. "It's not been

long enough. I came straight out here after doing the test. The instructions said to wait three minutes."

Three minutes. A hundred and eighty seconds. The difference between knowing and not knowing what the rest of his life entailed.

Knowing he was being a selfish bastard, he took a deep breath and clasped her hand. "Abs, I want you to know that regardless of what this test shows, I'll be here for you."

He didn't know how or what exactly he meant by his comment, but if he'd made her pregnant, he wouldn't abandon Abby. He might be a heartless bastard, but he'd do the right thing. Whatever the right thing was.

"I know you will." She sounded on the verge of tears. Her hand trembled and he clasped her fingers more tightly.

"If it's positive, I'll do whatever you want." What would she want? Marriage? An abortion? Child support? To castrate him for being so stupid as to get her pregnant?

"Okay, Dirk. That's fine."

Her voice was so flat his gaze lifted to hers. Unshed tears shone there and her lower lip quivered. Her fingers shook. Her whole body shook. He squeezed her hand, hoping to offer reassurance and wishing like hell someone would reassure him.

"Aw, honey, don't cry." He'd done this to her. It was his fault they were sitting here, wondering if they'd created a life. If only he'd not instantly been attracted to Abby. If only he'd not let the death of that little girl and her mother get to him. If only he hadn't found such comfort in Abby's arms. Sweet solace like none he'd known since Sandra and Shelby's deaths.

He could "if only" all day to no avail. If onlys wouldn't help them. Not at this point.

He wiped his finger along Abby's cheek, catching a runaway teardrop. "It'll be okay. One way or the other, it will be all right," he promised, although he wasn't sure he believed his words.

If Abby was pregnant, nothing would be all right.

She stared at him, opened her mouth, but no words left her tremulous lips.

"I'm sorry, Abs. So sorry." He leaned over and kissed her, gently, hoping to make the trembling stop, reminding himself that this was what had caused what they currently faced. Still, he wasn't able to stop.

Her mouth was warm and pliant, accepting his kiss, accepting him despite the fact he didn't deserve her.

"Oh, Abs, what have I done to you?" he whispered against her lips, threading his fingers into the soft waves of her hair.

"You didn't do anything to me, Dirk," she assured him, her voice catching slightly. "Nothing I didn't want."

"You didn't want this," he scoffed, gesturing toward the pregnancy kit.

"No, I didn't." She pulled back from him. Her eyes glistened with tears, but he'd never seen her look more sure of herself. "Not like this. Never like this. But if that test is positive, I will be okay."

"You'll keep the baby?"

She nodded.

"I'm sorry."

She stared him in the eyes, overflowing tears silently streaming down her cheeks. "For?"

"This. Taking advantage of you that morning."

"You didn't take advantage of me any more than I took advantage of you. We needed each other."

"What we did shouldn't have happened," he reminded her, so why was he holding her, leaning in to press another kiss to a teardrop on her cheek?

"No," she agreed, "but it did happen and we can't change the past."

"Or the consequences of that past." If only he could. Damn, there he went with another if only.

"True." She sighed, closing her eyes, opening them with strong resolve replacing her tears. "A baby wouldn't be the end of the world. Regardless of what the test shows, I will make the best of what life gives me."

She would, too. Dirk could see the determination and willpower reflected in her eyes. Knew enough about her to know Abby always made the best of any situation life presented. She was a glass half-full kind of woman.

Dirk had moved beyond glass half-empty years ago. His glass had been drained dry the moment his wife and daughter had taken their last breaths. After that, he'd tossed the cup against the wall, shattering the remains to bits.

"That's big of you, considering you're talking about the rest of your life." He couldn't keep the pain out of his voice. "A child is a big responsibility."

An odd expression on her face, Abby searched his eyes. "The biggest, really." She gripped his hand tightly in hers, a glimmer of uncertainty surfacing. "Promise me you'll try to be happy, too. Maybe it's crazy, but I need to hear you say that before we know, Dirk. Please."

Happy? She had no idea what she was asking

of him. How could he be happy if he'd made her pregnant? He'd given all his love to his wife and a beautiful little girl with straw-colored hair and big blue eyes, and that love had been ripped from his soul. He couldn't do that again.

When he didn't answer, Abby sighed, dropped her forehead against his. "Maybe it'll be negative and all of this will have been for nothing. It's probably been three minutes."

Dirk was sure it had, but he didn't move away from where he stared into Abby's eyes. He wasn't a fool. He could see that she did need to hear him say he'd try to be happy. He didn't understand why, couldn't begin to fathom why, but in her eyes he saw beyond the happy front she put on to the world and saw real need. Need unlike any he'd ever experienced. Need that made him feel emotionally impotent and protective at the same time. Abby's need gutted him.

The thought of disappointing her filled him with mixed emotions. She was the kind of woman a man felt inclined to protect, a sweet, wonderful, generous woman who gave a hundred and ten percent of herself to those in her life.

She'd welcomed him into her bed when he'd needed her.

Sex with her had been phenomenal and had provided his first moments of peace in years. Yet he'd known Abby didn't give her body lightly, that if they continued, she might fall for him and want things he didn't.

But whether or not he wanted those things, if Abby was pregnant, he'd be forced to accept what fate dealt him.

She wanted him to say he'd try to be happy if the test was positive, if she was pregnant with his baby.

He couldn't do it.

"You read the test," she urged, her eyes searching his.

Without a word, he picked up the test, registered the unmistakable plus sign and felt his stomach drop down the chimney lickety-split. "You're pregnant."

"I am?" Abby grabbed the test from his hand, studied the results. "I'm pregnant."

He'd said that.

"I'm pregnant, Dirk." Dropping the test back onto the coffee table as if the plastic had scalded her hand, she turned to him, wide-eyed and stunned, grabbed his hands and squeezed. "We're going to have a baby."

A baby. What could he say? He couldn't hurt Abby, couldn't suggest they consider their options, because even if he could ask, she wouldn't do that. He didn't have to hear the words to know that.

"Oh, God, I'm going to have a baby." Her chest rose and fell rapidly. Her eyes grew bigger and bigger. Her face grew paler and paler, as if she was on the verge of a panic attack. "What am I going to do with a baby?"

"You'll be fine." Had that really been his voice? Had he really sounded normal? He didn't feel normal. He felt as if he'd been dipped in ice water and stuck to the North Pole.

"Other than from nursing school, I don't know

anything about babies. Nothing." Was she even talking to him? Or just thinking out loud? Talking to herself?

She grabbed his arm, shook it as if to get his attention. "What if I don't know how to take care of him or her? Then what?"

"You'll be fine," he repeated, unable to think of anything better. Unable to think, period. Abby was pregnant. With his baby. He was going to be a father again. He didn't want another baby.

Yet he couldn't look away from Abby's pleading eyes, couldn't shut out the need he saw there.

But he wanted to. He wanted to run from her Christmas-filled house and never look back. Never have to face the fact that he'd fathered another child when he didn't have a heart to love him or her with.

Leaving Oak Park to escape his family and friends this holiday season had backfired. He'd jumped out of the frying pan and into the fire.

He pulled his hands free, turned from her to stare at her Christmas tree. God, he hated Christmas. Hated having to dredge up the past, but since she was having his baby, there were things Abby needed to know. Things she wouldn't like. By the time he was finished, she wouldn't like him. Which was fine. He hadn't liked himself in a long, long time either.

"I was married."

CHAPTER EIGHT

"Married?" Jack Frost zapped a frigid coating of ice over Abby's spine. Surely she'd heard Dirk wrong. Hadn't she been thinking earlier about how little she really knew about him? For all she knew, he could still have a wife and family back in Oak Park where he'd come from.

How could she be pregnant by a virtual stranger?

Only when he'd kissed her, made love to her, he hadn't been a stranger. Far, far from it. He'd known her better than anyone, had touched her soul right along with her body. She'd looked at him and felt she'd known the essence of who he was, all she'd needed to know.

But she hadn't. She hadn't known he'd been married.

She was pregnant. Dirk had been married. Why

wasn't he saying more? Why was he sitting there with his hands tightly fisted in his lap, with his jaw clenched and his eyes glazed over as if he were fighting demons? Had his marriage been that bad?

Was. That meant he wasn't still married, right? Why wasn't he explaining his bombshell statement?

"You were married?" she prompted.

He took a deep breath, raked his fingers through his hair. "Sandra and I married too young. I was still in medical school, gone most of the time, didn't have two nickels to rub together, but we loved each other. Then Shelby came into the picture."

Another layer of ice settled over Abby's nerves.

"Shelby?" Was she a girlfriend? A mistress? A brief fling he'd had on the side? A—?

"My daughter."

His daughter? Abby blinked, sure she'd heard wrong. He had a daughter? Why hadn't he mentioned a daughter? How could she have not known such pertinent details?

Then again, why would she have known? She wasn't important to Dirk. Why would he have told her? Disgust filled her. How could she have been so foolish?

Outside work she'd spent a total of four—*four!*—days with him. The day she'd gotten pregnant, his Santa stint, the Christmas party, and today, the day they'd found out she was pregnant.

God, what must he think of her?

Then again, she hadn't been alone in that bed. She refused to abide by some double standard that said it was okay for him to sleep with a woman he barely knew, but that for her to do the same made her less of a woman.

He had a daughter. A wife, hopefully former wife, but the fact he'd not clarified that point worried her. He had a whole other life she knew nothing about. A whole other life he hadn't shared with her. Would he ever have if she hadn't gotten pregnant?

God, she was going to throw up.

"Do your wife and Shelby live in Oak Park?"

She asked each word slowly, controlling each breath to keep from gasping air into her aching chest.

Was that why she occasionally saw the look of pain in his eyes when he treated a child? Was that why he never seemed completely comfortable in a child's presence? Because seeing children made him miss his daughter? Had he and his wife had problems? She should have suspected something the moment he admitted to not liking Christmas!

"No, Sandra and Shelby don't live in Oak Park. They don't live anywhere." His voice caught, his jaw flexed, he swallowed. "They died in a car accident four years ago. Shelby was only two years old."

"Oh, God." Which explained why he'd reacted so emotionally on the day they'd made love. The mother and daughter dying in the car accident must have stirred up memories of his own losses. Dirk had had a daughter who'd died. A wife who'd died. Abby's heart twisted inside out at the thought of how much that must hurt, at what he'd been through. "I'm so sorry, Dirk."

She placed her hand over his, hoping he sensed how she wanted to comfort him.

"It's not your fault." He pulled his hand free, raked his fingers through his hair, looked tormented, as if he was erecting every defensive wall around himself. "Just as this pregnancy isn't your fault. I'm the one who's sorry."

She had a thousand questions, things she wanted to know, to understand him better, really know this man whose baby grew inside her. But he'd closed his eyes and, she suspected, the subject of his past as well.

Still, she ached for him and, as awkward as she felt doing so given their current predicament, she wrapped her arms around him and gave him a hug. A big hug. She held on to him, hoping he knew how much she wanted to ease his burden. He sat stock still, never moving, never budging, never talking. Just sat.

"I don't blame you for my pregnancy," she assured him, "if that's what you're wondering.

We're both consenting adults. We used protection. Neither of us could have known this would happen."

She traced her finger over his, laced their hands. Although she wasn't sure he welcomed her hold, she squeezed. "We'll figure this out, Dirk. Somehow, all this will work out okay."

But even as she said the words, Abby wondered if they were true. Wondered why she was having to play the role of the strong one when really she just wanted to curl up against him and cry. She wanted his arms to be wrapped around her, to have him holding her, giving comfort. She wanted to be the one taken care of, the one who got to let her emotions loose, and be comforted.

Instead, she'd be raising a baby, possibly by herself, and would never have the dreams she'd clung to since childhood.

Dreams of magical Christmases with a man who loved her and their happy family. Dreams of someday sharing the magical news of a pregnancy with a life partner who would rejoice with her at the news. Dreams of a happily ever after written just for her and her special Prince Charming.

From the first, she'd hoped Dirk would be that man, but not under these circumstances. Unable to hold back the erupting emotional volcano, Abby burst into tears.

And although Dirk wrapped his arms loosely around her, she found no solace in his embrace.

How could she when he was only holding her because he was trying to do the right thing and not because he loved her or wanted her pregnant with his child?

Did Dirk really think no one was going to suspect something was up when he kept babying her? *Argh*. Abby was going to strangle him if didn't quit treating her so differently. Their co-workers weren't stupid.

And neither was she. After the halfhearted way he'd held her while she'd cried, she'd known she had to protect herself. After he'd left, she'd cried more, this time for the great grief rocking her insides, grief that she'd entangled her emotions so irreversibly with a man incapable of returning her sentiments. Even if he wanted to, he'd locked his heart away years ago and thrown away the key.

Dirk was a good man, but one without a heart to give, which meant she needed to guard hers with all her being.

"Here, let me do that." He stepped into her personal space, taking over where she was helping to transfer a patient from a gurney onto an exam table.

Biting her tongue because she didn't want to draw more attention to what he was doing, she shot him a back-off look and tried to continue with her job, to no avail since he didn't step away as they vied for a hold on the patient.

As their coworkers were looking back and forth between them, and even the patient had a curious look on her face, Abby held up her hands.

"Fine, Dr. Kelley. I'll go check on bay three's

X-ray report." At least she sounded professional, even if he was making her look like an invalid.

What was wrong with him anyway? Why was he acting like she couldn't do a thing for herself without his help? She was pregnant, not disabled.

"He's quite taken with you, isn't he?"

Abby spun to look at the medical assistant who'd only been working at the hospital for a few weeks. "Who?"

The girl, who couldn't be much older than high-school age, smiled. "Dr. Kelley, of course. I saw you together at the Christmas party. You make a lovely couple."

Abby swallowed the lump in her throat. She'd thought they made a lovely couple, too. Now, she knew they'd never be a couple. Perhaps if they'd had more time prior to her pregnancy, perhaps if they'd met years ago, before Dirk's marriage. Now it was too late.

"We're not a couple."

Dirk didn't do couples. Just because she was pregnant it did not mean she expected that to change. Neither did she want it to change because of her pregnancy.

She wanted Dirk to care enough for her to want to be a couple with her. Because of her. Because of his feelings for her.

She wanted him to love her.

The young girl frowned. "Really? I'm surprised. You looked like you were having a good time together."

That had been before they'd been interrupted and he'd said he wanted to just be friends. Before they'd known they were going to be parents. Before she'd realized Dirk was incapable of giving his heart to her.

"We were having a good time. As friends."

"Oh." The assistant didn't look as if she knew what else to say.

"No problem," she assured the girl, keeping an "it's no big deal" smile on her face in the hope of waylaying more curiosity. Particularly in light of Dirk's odd behavior since she'd clocked in. "Do you know if the X-ray reports are back on the fall patient in the next bay?"

Looking chastised, although Abby hadn't meant her to, the girl nodded. "They are."

No wonder the girl had thought they were a couple as they'd left in such a heated rush from the Christmas party and with the way Dirk had acted tonight.

She really was going to have it out with him the first private moment they got. Although they'd have to establish some type of relationship for the future, his overbearing, almost paternalistic attitude had to go. Besides, for now, Abby wanted a break from him. Later, after the holidays had passed, she'd figure out how she and Dirk could coexist in the world of parenthood.

"Hello, Mrs. Clifton," she greeted her patient, a friendly smile pasted on her face in the hope of reassuring the woman. "Dr. Kelley will be by in a few minutes to give your X-ray results." She pulled up the tests and flagged them for his attention. "How are you feeling?"

"Foolish." The woman in her early sixties gestured to the arm she held very still. "I still can't believe I slipped and did this."

"Unfortunately, falls happen." Abby lightly pinched each of the woman's fingertips, observing how quickly the blanched skin returned to its natural pink color. Almost immediately. Excellent.

"I guess this will teach me to be more careful of ice." The woman shifted, trying to get comfortable.

"Who knows, this might save you a much worse accident later down the line." Abby checked the automatic blood-pressure cuff that was wrapped around the woman's uninjured arm. One twenty-six over seventy-eight. Great. A normal reading.

The woman laughed lightly. "You're one of those positive people who always sees the best in everything, aren't you?"

"Usually." Only she hadn't been seeing the positive in her pregnancy. Only the negative. Only that her dreams for her future were undergoing a drastic transformation.

She was going to have a baby. A beautiful, precious baby that she and Dirk had made together.

A baby to share her life with. To be a family with. To share Christmas with. Abby had never met anyone other than Dirk who she'd want to have a baby with. No one she'd want to share the rest of her Christmases with. Just Dirk.

If they weren't meant to be more than friends, then she'd deal with that, would love and cherish their baby without letting Dirk break her heart. Somehow.

"Nurse?" Mrs. Clifton eyed her curiously.

Pulling her thoughts together, Abby smiled at the elderly lady. "Thank you."

The woman's forehead creased. "What for?"

"For reminding me that it's much too wonderful a season to be down."

Especially over something that so many women would consider a blessing. She'd been given a gift, an unexpected, unplanned-for gift, but a gift all the same.

Just because that gift hadn't come at the time in her life she'd planned or in the way she'd hoped for didn't make a baby any less of a blessing.

Yes, there was still that part of her that didn't

want this, wanted her and Dirk to have the opportunity to get to know each other without a pregnancy shadowing their every thought and word. She didn't have that luxury.

She was going to be mother to Dirk's child.

"Were you down?"

Abby considered the question. "Not really. I just wasn't seeing the miracles of Christmas clearly."

"Christmas is the best time of year, isn't it?" Her patient's gaze fell on her immobilized arm. "Only this year someone else will have to do the cooking because I suspect I'm not going to be doing much of anything."

Helping reposition her pillow, Abby nodded her agreement. "I suspect you're right. I hope you have your shopping finished."

"Mercifully, yes. I'm one of those crazy women who gets up before dawn and does all my shopping on the day after Thanksgiving." The woman chuckled self-derisively. "Fighting the crowds is a bit rough at times, but the bargain buys are worth the effort."

"Aren't they just the best? I do the same thing."

Dirk stepped into the area, his face going pale.

Abby bit back a sigh. Did he really dislike Christmas so much that just hearing a discussion about shopping bothered him? How would she explain to her child that his or her father didn't like Christmas?

Avoiding looking at him, Abby entered her nurse's notes while Dirk went over the X-ray results with Mrs. Clifton, explaining that she needed to schedule an appointment with her primary care provider in addition to seeing the orthopedic surgeon the following day.

He left the room long enough to grab some patient education materials, flipped the pamphlet open to a page with a photo of magnified images of a normal bone and an osteoporotic one.

"Your arm broke more easily than it should have because your bones are thinning due to a condition called osteoporosis," Dirk explained, pointing out the difference in the bones in the pictures. "This happens when the bones lose mass, weakening, leaving them in a state where it takes much less force to cause a fracture. Sometimes even something as simple as taking a step can cause the bones to crush in on themselves when the bones have weakened."

"Crush in on themselves? The bones can break without me even falling?"

"Yes, it's possible in osteoporosis, but falling or taking a hit is much more likely to be the culprit of a break."

"I have this?"

"You do." He nodded. "Have you ever been told you have osteoporosis?"

"At my last physical, my nurse practitioner mentioned that I should be taking calcium." The woman gave a guilty shrug. "She tried to get me to go onto a medication to make my bones stronger."

Dirk's brow lifted. "Tried?"

The woman sighed, shrugged her good shoulder. "The medicine gave me bad indigestion so I only took a couple of doses."

Dirk frowned. "Did you let her know you'd stopped taking the medication?"

She shook her head, careful not to disturb her arm. "No, I figured I'd discuss it with her at my next visit." She gave him a thoughtful look. "If I'd been taking the medicine, would my bone have broken from falling tonight?"

"It's impossible to know for sure," Dirk replied. "Medications can add around ten percent back to the bone strength, which is a significant amount and can mean the difference between a break and no break." He pointed to the X-rays again. "The medicine rebuilds those tiny connections, adding strength. With bones as thin as yours are, you do need to be on some type of bisphosphonate."

"Putting up with a little heartburn would have been better than this." She gestured to her immobilized arm.

"You should discuss your options with your nurse practitioner. There are a wide range of treatments for osteoporosis, including a once-a-year intravenous infusion of medication. With the IV method, you wouldn't have to worry about taking a pill or having indigestion as that alternative would bypass that system and the side effects of pills."

The woman asked a few more questions which Dirk patiently answered. Watching him, watching his seemingly infinite patience when the woman became repetitious in her efforts to understand, gave Abby insight to Dirk. She'd witnessed his patience, his kindness, his caring time and again in the emergency room while he dealt with patients from all walks of life. Not once had he lost his temper or behaved unprofessionally.

She didn't have to wonder if he'd been a good father. He had. Although, no doubt, with completing his residency, he'd probably been so busy that he'd missed out on more of his daughter's short life than he'd have liked. Sandra Kelley had been a lucky woman to have Dirk's love, to have had his baby, and experience the joys of pregnancy and motherhood with Dirk by her side, loving her.

Despite his aversion to Christmas, Dirk was a good man. The best Abby had ever met, really.

Honest, honorable, giving, strong in character.

Why didn't he like Christmas? Did the holidays remind him of all he'd lost? Of Christmases he'd shared with his wife and young daughter?

Would she and their child forever live in the shadow of his former life? God, she prayed not, but deep down she wondered if that wouldn't be the case.

If that happened, how would she prevent that overshadowing their child's well-being? Just the thought of their child being made to feel inferior made her neck muscles ache and her stomach clench.

She finished her notes, left the bay and entered the next, determined to stay on task. A patient she'd triaged had discovered a large amount of blood in their urine and had been having tremendous back pain. She'd put him into the bay, and initiated protocol hematuria labs.

When Dirk stepped out of the fractured

arm patient's bay, Abby caught him and without meeting his eyes gave him the stats on the patient. "Do you want to get a renal protocol CT scan?"

"Yes. Thanks." When she started to walk away, he grabbed her wrist, causing her to turn to look at him. "You holding up okay? You're not overdoing it, are you?"

That did it. She'd had enough of him interfering with her work.

"No." She pulled her arm free, hoping no one noticed. "My back hurts. My feet hurt. I'm tired. My stomach hasn't felt right in days. But the main reason I'm not holding up is *you*."

His forehead wrinkled. "Me?"

"You're driving me crazy. You've got to stop treating me differently than you were before, well, you know."

His jaw worked back and forth slowly, as if he was trying to categorize her words and having difficulty knowing where to stick them. "I'm concerned."

"I appreciate your concern, but work isn't the

place. I've got a job to do and if you keep making a difference, people are going to complain."

"People?"

"Our coworkers."

"I don't care what anyone thinks, except you, Abby."

He was saying all the right things, but Abby didn't want to hear them, could only hear his "let's just be friends" speech echoing through her head. She didn't want or need his overbearing behavior.

In his "concern," he was exposing her to her colleagues' curiosity. Her volunteer friends suspecting she was pregnant was one thing. Her coworkers another matter entirely. Not that they wouldn't know soon enough.

Everyone would know soon enough.

But she wanted a few weeks of having the knowledge to herself, to completely come to terms with her future plans prior to having to answer other people's questions.

"Well, I do care." It wasn't asking too much for him to give her time to work through this in privacy. "A lot of my closest friends work here. I won't have you undermining me."

His gaze narrowed. "No one would say anything if you needed an extra break."

Abby's jaw dropped. "Why wouldn't they?"

He looked away, guiltily, not answering her. "Dirk?"

When his eyes met hers, a bit of arrogance she hadn't previously witnessed shone there. "I'm a doctor, Abby. If I give a nurse permission to take an extra break because I think she needs one, no one is going to deny that right."

Oh, no. That so wasn't going to happen. He'd do irreparable damage to her working environment. With a baby on the way, she needed her job.

"I can't take extra breaks just because you think I should." She paused, acutely aware they stood in the busy emergency room. No one was near them, but when Abby glanced around, the medical assistant was watching them curiously, a "yeah right, just friends" expression on her young face. "We can't discuss this here. Just let me do my job, okay? That's all I ask."

"Abby—"

"Dr. Kelley," an assistant interrupted, looking back and forth between them. "There's a myocardial infarction patient on his way in. The ambulance is en route and should arrive in two minutes."

Grateful for the interruption, Abby jumped into action. "I'll get the renal protocol CT scan entered into the computer and have everything ready for the MI arrival."

"Abby—"

"Take care of your patients, Dr. Kelley, and leave me alone. I can take care of myself and don't need or want your *friendship* after all." With that she spun on her heel and walked away from a man capable of breaking her heart.

When the paramedics rushed the man in, a team was ready in the emergency room to take over trying to save the man's life.

Abby stayed busy for the rest of her shift, working straight through her break, grateful for the mental reprieve from her personal life due to the intensity of their patients' needs.

Definitely meeting Danielle's definition of brooding, Dirk never said another word outside anything to do with their patients. However, when he realized she'd not taken a break, not eaten, he'd disappeared and come back with a cup of yogurt, bottled water and an apple, thrust them toward her and walked away without uttering a single word.

His expression hadn't been a pleased one. Actually, he'd looked irritated.

Part of her had wanted to toss the items at the back of his retreating, arrogant head. He deserved a good wake-up thwack. How dared he be so high-handed? Just because she was pregnant it did not give him the right to dictate what she should and shouldn't do. He'd said he just wanted to be friends, giving up any potential right to have a say in her life.

She was her own woman, could do this on her own, would forge a good life for her and her baby.

Abby desperately clung to that thought as a shield against the hurt Dirk's rejection had caused.

Clung to her mounting anger at his hot-cold attitude to prevent more pain from seeping through and jabbing at her vulnerable heart.

CHAPTER NINE

IF ABBY didn't open her door soon, Dirk was going to jemmy the lock. Or break down the door.

Was this his fourth round of knocks or his fifth?

Where was she?

Finally, he heard a scratching at the other side of the door. At least Mistletoe was up and about. Abby should be, too. If she'd gone home and gone to bed, she'd have had a good eight hours.

Was she okay? She'd looked so tired and pale when she'd left the hospital and hadn't acted like her normal self. He'd been tied up with a patient when she'd clocked out, hadn't been able to believe she'd left without telling him she was going.

As if she was truly angry with him. He'd have

understood anger on the day they'd found out she was pregnant, would have understood if she'd beat his chest with her fists, but last night? Hell, he'd made a conscious effort to take care of her, to let her know he planned to be there for her and their baby even if the mere thought gave him hives. Didn't she understand how difficult this was for him? How hard he was trying?

The lock clicked, and the door swung open. Abby squinted, putting her hand up to block the fading sunlight filtering onto the porch. "Dirk? What are you doing here?"

"You look awful."

Standing in her doorway wearing baggy sweats, her hair wild, dark shadows bruising her eyes, Abby did look awful. Like she hadn't gone to bed after leaving work.

"Nice to see you, too," she mumbled. Her cat rubbing against her leg, meowing, she moved aside for Dirk to enter.

Carrying a bag of groceries he'd brought because he seriously doubted she was taking care of herself, he stepped into her foyer. He eyed her more closely, taking in the pallor of her skin, the redness in her eyes. "Did you volunteer somewhere after work this morning?"

She shut her front door, turned to face him. "You're not my boss. Not outside the emergency room. If I want to volunteer somewhere, I can."

"Which means you did." He let out an exasperated sigh, assessing her like a bug under a magnifying glass. "Why didn't you tell me? I would have gone with you."

"Have you considered that maybe I didn't tell you because I didn't want you to go?" She yawned, stretched her arms over her head, raising the shapeless sweat shirt up to expose a tiny sliver of ivory skin.

"No, I haven't considered that. Why wouldn't you want my help?" Forcing his gaze away from that glimpse of flesh, Dirk swallowed, shifted the groceries in his arms. How could he be looking at her one minute, thinking how tired she looked and wanting to throttle her for not taking better care of herself and the next be fighting the desire to pull that sweatshirt over her head to expose a whole lot more of her delectable body?

"Go away, Dirk," she continued, gratefully oblivious to the effect her stretch had had on his body and mind.

"No." After a few minutes of lying in his bed, thinking about Abby and her uncharacteristic snippiness, he had crashed into a dreamless sleep and awakened with only one thought. Seeing Abby, making sure she was okay. "You need someone to look after you."

"I can look after myself just fine." Her lower lip puckered in an almost pout.

His gaze zeroed in on that full bottom lip. He wanted to kiss her. To take her in his arms and kiss her until she sighed in contentment.

"Since when?" Dirk fought wincing at how brusque his tone was. Just because he was fighting sexual awareness he shouldn't be feeling when she looked exhausted, it didn't mean she'd understand that's what was causing his irritation. What was it about the woman that drove him so physically crazy? Taking a deep breath, he tried again in a calmer tone. "You pulled an exhausting twelve-hour shift, Abby. What was so important that you couldn't have rested first? Something to do with Christmas again?"

Mixed emotions flashed across her face, mostly irritation. "Just because you don't understand my love of Christmas, it doesn't mean you get to prioritize my activities. Volunteering is important to me."

Shifting the grocery bag, he gave her an exasperated look. "What about our baby's well-being? Doesn't that count for something?"

"I'm not going to dignify that with an answer." Turning away, she walked over to the sofa, sat and wrapped a blanket around herself. The same blanket she'd wrapped around her almost naked body just a few nights ago.

Dirk swallowed. Hard.

"Christmas makes me happy." She looked like a vulnerable child, one he wanted to take into his arms and hold. But she wasn't a child. And if she were in his arms, he'd want much more than to hold her. She was a grown woman, a woman who he'd thought about almost non-stop since the night they'd met, a woman he desperately wanted. Why did he get the feeling Christmas meant more to Abby than the obvious?

"Look, you don't have to check on me just because I'm pregnant." She pulled the blanket more tightly around herself, causing the cat, which had jumped up next to her, to look annoyed. She picked up the fat cat, placing the animal in her lap and stroking her fingers over his fur. "Actually, I'd prefer it if you didn't."

"Why not?" He moved into her line of sight, but didn't sit down, just stood, watching her, wondering why she was shutting him out. His reaction on the day they'd found out she was pregnant hadn't been the greatest, but the news had caught him off guard. Way off guard. He'd have sworn she understood, that she didn't want a baby any more than he did. Finding out she was having a baby, that the rest of her life was going to be vastly different than she'd thought couldn't have been any easier for her than it had been for him. Probably, the news had been more stressful to her. But he was trying. He was concerned, wanted what was best for her and their baby. Why was she being so difficult?

"We're not a couple, Dirk. We weren't before this and we aren't now," she pointed out, scratching behind her cat's ears. "People are getting the wrong idea."

"What?" Was she serious? "How could they get the wrong idea? You're pregnant with my baby."

"Neither of us wanted this baby."

He winced. What she said was true, and yet to hear the words come out of her sweet lips so bluntly felt wrong. He'd never considered having more children, never considered starting over. He didn't want to start over, but neither did he want to father an unwanted child.

"Whether or not we want to be parents, Abby, we're going to be. We have to do what's best for the baby." God, he sounded so logical, so clinical. Did she have any idea how awkward this was for him? Standing above her, holding the groceries he'd brought to make her something to eat, her refusing to even look at him.

Her gaze remained fixed on where she petted her purring cat, her long fingers stroking back and forth. Lucky cat.

"I'm not stupid, Dirk. I will do what's best for the baby. But for now I want time."

"We don't have to tell anyone for a while, but you won't be able to hide your pregnancy for long, Abby. Decisions will have to be made. Soon."

Looking unsure for the first time since he'd arrived, she pulled her knees up, dropped her head onto them, burying her face in the folds of the blanket. "I hate this."

Helplessness washed over him. She looked so alone, so stressed. He wanted to take her into his arms, to hold her and never let go. But he just stood there. Taking her into his arms would accomplish what? Other than send his libido through the roof? Besides, he wasn't so sure she'd welcome his embrace.

As if sensing his thoughts, sensing his need

for her to look at him, she glanced up with red-rimmed, watery eyes. "You seem to be handling this fairly well this morning."

Dirk felt as if a string of Christmas lights had been twisted around his throat and cut off his air supply.

Looks could be deceiving. He wasn't handling anything. But not wanting to deal with something didn't mean one could just ignore life's realities. He'd learned that lesson well.

"There's really no choice. Which means we have to make plans."

She inhaled deeply and let her breath out slowly. "Plans?"

"To protect you and the baby."

"No." Her jaw dropped and she shook her head in short little jerks. "I'm not going to marry you, Dirk. Don't even ask. That would just be compounding our mistakes and, honestly, if you did I think…well, just don't."

Ouch. She had a way of striking beneath his armor. "I didn't plan to ask you to marry me, Abby.

Although if that's what you wanted, I wouldn't deny your request under the circumstances."

"My request? Under the circumstances?" She snorted. "I'm pregnant, Dirk. Not dying. I'm a big girl. I can take care of myself and this baby, too. I don't need you."

Did she think he'd just walk away and forget she was having his baby? Then the truth hit him. For all her bravado, Abby was scared. She did want his concern, but didn't know the first thing about accepting that concern. He'd gotten the impression her family had been close before her parents' deaths. What had happened to her after that? Had she been taken care of? Loved?

"Yes," he said softly, "you do."

She glanced up again. Surprise flickered in her eyes. "How dare you presume you know what I need? You know nothing about me."

He knew she was a prickly little thing when she was on the defensive. But why was she on the defensive with him? It just didn't feel right. Didn't she know she could trust him? That he'd never hurt her?

What was that she'd said at the Christmas party?

Maybe not intentionally.

She'd been right. He had hurt her. They just hadn't known it at the time. But he refused to accept her assessment that he knew nothing about her.

"I know more than you think. You're a great nurse. A caring woman. A fantastic lover." Her lower lip disappeared into her mouth, vulnerability shining so brightly in her eyes it almost blinded him. "And I believe you're going to be a great mother to our baby."

The tears Abby had been fighting pricked her eyes. How dared he come into her house and spout off sweet words like that after the awful morning she'd spent tossing and turning on the sofa? The sofa because she hadn't been able to get comfortable in her bed, had given up and curled up in the living room, staring at her mother's Christmas village pieces, wishing she could lose herself in that happy little world. Finally, she'd dozed a little.

She loved nursing and liked to believe he was right, that she was a great nurse. She could also go with the caring woman. She did care about others. But a fantastic lover? What a joke.

"We both know I wasn't a fantastic lover." She snorted softly at the mere idea of him thinking her fantastic. Not that he'd complained but, still, she doubted she'd been fantastic or anywhere close.

"Yes, you were, Abby." He set the bag on her coffee table, squatted next to her and reached for her hand.

"So fantastic you couldn't run away fast enough." She stuck her hands under the blanket, anywhere to keep him from touching her. She couldn't think when he did that. Not that she was thinking clearly anyway. Not after discovering she was going to be a mother, not sleeping much, and crying a whole lot.

He touched her anyway, running his fingers along the side of her face, into the edges of her wild-about-her-head hair. "So fantastic just re-membering takes my breath away."

Why did she want to lean against him? To toss the blanket away and fall into his arms and cry until there were no more tears left?

"Why are you here, Dirk?" she asked, wishing he'd go, would leave her to what so far had been a less than stellar day. "Just go home."

"Can't do," he said, shaking the burgeon-ing plastic bag he'd put on the coffee table. "I brought you breakfast. Or lunch." He glanced at his wristwatch. "Or dinner. Whatever you want to call it. Regardless, I'm going to make you a healthy meal."

Just the thought of breakfast made her stomach heave. She grimaced. "Food is the last thing I want right now."

"You have to eat."

She rolled her eyes. "What would be the point?"

He stared at her for long moments and when she met his gaze, his were so intent she couldn't look away even though she desperately wanted to.

"Abby, you've got to stop arguing with me."

She bit the inside of her lip. "Who's arguing?"

Stroking his fingers along the side of her face, he sighed. "This is certainly a side of you I've never seen."

She was sure it was a side he wished he still hadn't seen. Unbrushed hair, makeup-less face, nauseated-all-morning pallor. She wouldn't win any beauty prizes on her best days. Today she might send small children running for the hills.

"No one invited you here or is making you stay," she reminded him, chin lifting.

But rather than take offense at her unusual surliness, he just smiled, as if he knew some secret she didn't.

"Go take a shower. You'll feel better." Another of those dazzling smiles that it really wasn't fair for him to be flashing when she felt so… What was it she felt? Hadn't she decided the other night at the hospital that their baby was a gift? One that she'd treasure? But right now Dirk's smile, his gorgeous face and body, just annoyed her. How dared he look so wonderful when she felt so awful?

"I'll slice fresh fruit and cook breakfast." He leaned forward, dropped a kiss at her temple, lingered a brief moment.

Oh, my. If she didn't know better she'd swear he was breathing in her scent.

"How do you like your eggs, Abby?" Oh, he'd definitely nuzzled her just then, his hot breath caressing her cheek, burning her all the way down to her toes.

"Have you not heard a word I've said? I don't want breakfast. I don't want a shower." Well, a long shower would be nice and the hot water might ease her achy body. "I just want to be left alone."

He cupped her face, holding her gaze to his. "No."

Abby gawked, not believing his high-handedness. "No?"

"I'm not leaving, Abby." This time his lips

brushed her face, trailing light kisses on her cheek. "Not when you're like this."

Shivering from his touch, she took a deep breath. "Like what? I'm fine."

He didn't laugh, but he could have. She was so far from fine that no one would have thought less of him if he'd had a good chuckle at her comment. She felt on the verge of screaming, crying, laughing hysterically, throwing herself into his arms and begging him to love her, an entire plethora of heightened emotions all surging at once through her hormonal system.

"It's going to be okay, Abby." He brushed her hair away from her face, stared into her eyes and warmed a place deep inside her that she hadn't realized had chilled the moment he'd said she was pregnant. "I'm as scared as you are about this, but somehow this is all going to be okay. We'll make it okay. Together."

When his lips covered hers, she let herself believe him. Let herself give in to the temptation of his touch, the warmth of his caresses, the power of the emotions between them.

She couldn't exactly recall how Mistletoe ended up in the floor and Dirk stretched out above her, his weight pressing her into the sofa, his mouth drawing out her every breath. She clung to him, loving the weight of him covering her, loving his strength, the need in his kisses, his touches.

Rather than the frantic way they'd made love on that morning, or even their desperation the night of the Christmas party, their touches were slower, more drawn out, more *everything*.

Her brain screamed in protest, reminding her she was supposed to be protecting her heart against him, not kissing him, not helping as he pulled her sweatshirt over her head, revealing her naked breasts to his eager inspection. His eager kisses.

"I want you, Abby," he breathed from between her breasts. "Let me love you."

Despite knowing she should stop him, should not expose her all too vulnerable heart, she couldn't deny Dirk, not when his hot mouth felt so good on her body, not when she suspected he already owned her heart. All of her heart.

She wanted his love. More than she'd ever dreamed of wanting anything in her whole life, she wanted this man. All of him. His mind, his body, his heart. Yes, she definitely wanted Dirk's heart.

She tugged his T-shirt free, helped pull the material over his head, bit back a groan at the beauty of his naked torso. He removed his jeans, her sweats, and was inside her in what seemed a single breath. No condom. What would be the point? Body to body. Soul to soul.

"Abby," he breathed against her mouth, staring into her eyes, moving inside her. "I'm not going to last long. Not like this. I—I need you so much. So much."

Clasping her hands with his, he drove deeper, so deep Abby lost where she ended and he began, gave herself over to the emotions flooding through her body, her heart.

Not her heart, Dirk's.

If she'd had any doubts before, she no longer did. Her heart, all of her, belonged to him, completely and irrevocably.

She wrapped her legs around him, drawing him deeper, deeper still. "I need you, too."

Saying the words out loud somehow made them more real, somehow made her feel more vulnerable. But looking into his eyes, seeing matching need, real need, she could only expose herself further.

I love you.

She wasn't sure if she said the words out loud or just in her heart. Regardless, she felt them with all her soul, with everything she was.

She loved Dirk.

Much later, Abby didn't eat any of the turkey bacon Dirk fried, but she did have a healthy portion of the freshly sliced cantaloupe, scrambled eggs and buttered toast. And didn't dry heave once.

Amazing what good sex did for a body. Not good sex. *Great* sex.

No, not sex. No way could what they'd just shared be called mere sex. No, what they'd just done transcended everything.

"Apparently—" she smiled, feeling a little shy "—I like your cooking better than my own."

"Impossible." His grin was contagious, complete. Real. "I've had your fudge, Abby. You're a whiz in the kitchen."

"Thanks." She watched him feed Mistletoe the leftover bacon. The cat purred against his leg, brushing against him time and again. Mistletoe wasn't the only one wanting to rub against Dirk. "My cat will forever be begging for more."

Just like she worried she'd be begging for more of the attention he'd shown her this morning. Wow.

Lord help her! She loved him.

The man had cooked her breakfast, made wonderful love to her until they'd both cried out. Afterwards, he'd held her. Held her tightly to him, stroking his fingers across her belly. She'd wished she'd known what he'd been thinking, wished she'd known if his caress had been incidental or if he'd purposely touched her where their baby grew.

She stood, intending to help clear away the dishes, but Dirk motioned for her to sit.

"I'm pregnant, Dirk, not disabled. You cooked. I clean."

"No." He shook his head, pointing at her chair. "My treat."

Okay, part of her thrilled at the idea that he was pampering her. Had she ever been pampered in her life? She didn't think so. Not since her mom and dad had died.

"I can wash dirty dishes," she assured him, not wanting the way he'd treated her at work to extend into her home. She wasn't an invalid. "Besides, you really didn't make that much of a mess. It won't take but a jiffy to clean."

"Probably not, but today is my treat. Take a load off, Abby."

She stood next to her chair, eyeing him, yet again wishing she could read his thoughts. "Why?"

"What do you mean, why? Can't I do something nice for you without you questioning my motives?"

She bit into her lower lip. "Is it because you feel guilty?"

"I am guilty, but that's not why I'm here."

His blue eyes looked so sincere. "Then why?"

He leaned back in his chair, looked perplexed, then shrugged. "I want to spend time with you."

"Because I'm pregnant?"

He studied her a moment. "I've wanted to be with you from the moment we met, Abby. That's how you ended up pregnant."

"I'm pregnant because we had a horrible night in the E.R." She didn't remind him of the similarities to his own tragic losses. She understood why he hadn't wanted to be alone, forgave him for using her, found herself wanting to comfort him even more now that she understood why he'd been so deeply affected. But that wasn't what earlier had been about, was it?

"I've had horrible nights in the E.R. before and never slept with my nurse."

Why did that admission make her feel better, lighter, less used?

"If the attraction hadn't been so strong between us, no tragedy would have brought us together like that." His confident tone left no room for doubt. "I made love to you because I wanted to make love to you. Just as I wanted to make love to you today. When I look at you, I can't think about much of anything except having you."

Had he really just admitted that he wanted her? She'd thought so, but then the whole pregnancy issue had clouded her thinking yesterday and this morning. But he had wanted her. He'd said made love, not have comfort sex or one-night-stand sex or guilt sex.

"And now?" she asked, grabbing at the rope he was throwing her, hoping it was long enough to save her, hoping she wasn't grasping at straws. "Months went by with you barely acknowledging I existed outside work."

"I want you, if that's what you're asking. I never stopped wanting you. After what we just shared, surely you don't doubt that." His eyes caressed her face. "You're beautiful, Abby."

"You told me I looked awful," she reminded him.

"That was pre-shower." His tone was teasing, but his eyes remained dark, stormy. "You're always beautiful, Abby. You must know that."

"Thank you," she said. How could she not believe him when his gaze echoed his words? Dirk really did find her beautiful. He really did want her and really had made love to her.

Christmas miracles never ceased.

"But we can't repeat what just happened. Not when we're just friends."

She stood corrected.

Apparently, Christmas miracles did cease.

CHAPTER TEN

HAVING made it clear that he planned to lighten her load whether Abby wanted him to or not, Dirk went with her to her volunteer stints, becoming more and more involved in her day-to-day life, more and more involved in her Christmas charity events.

Although he didn't pretend the Christmas aspect didn't bother him, he no longer winced when she told him what they'd be doing for the day.

As she'd just done.

He'd come over, insisted upon bringing bagels, cream cheese and fresh fruit. They'd eaten and addressed Christmas cards to be distributed to nursing-home residents. When they'd finished, running his finger over the steepled church to her mother's Christmas village, Abby's favorite piece, he'd asked what was next.

"It's called Toys for Toddlers. Various businesses have set up stations for people to donate toys to be given as Christmas gifts to needy children. Our job is to go by the various drop-off points and pick up the toys. We'll deliver them to the headquarters and volunteers will wrap them at a later time, probably tomorrow."

His face remained impassive as he picked up a village figure of a couple holding hands on a park bench. "When and how do the toys actually get to the kids?"

Purposely trying to look impish, Abby smiled. "Santa delivers them, of course."

His gaze narrowed suspiciously and she'd swear he'd have tugged on his collar if he had one. She bit back laughter, enjoying teasing him, enjoying this budding aspect to their relationship.

"Santa?"

Watching as he carefully replaced the figure where she'd had it, she gave in. "No worries." She placed her hand on his arm, loved the sinewy strength there, but wondered at herself for touching him when she usually so carefully avoided doing so. "You're safe. I'm not in charge of Santa."

At least he was safe from playing Santa. Safe from her was another matter altogether. The contact of their skin touching was frying her brain cells, making her want to push him down on the sofa and leap into his lap for a little Santa role playing. She had all kinds of things on her wish list—naughty and nice.

She wanted him to kiss her, believed he wanted to kiss her, too. As frustrating as she found his insistence that they were just friends, she believed he had his reasons. But if he didn't work through them soon, she was going to make herself a mistletoe halo and wear it at all times.

"That's good to know." He sighed with real relief.

She observed him closely, noted that his shoulders had relaxed with her answer. "I was teasing. Maybe I shouldn't have, but I couldn't resist. Was being my Santa really that bad?"

He closed his eyes and took a deep breath.

When he spoke, his voice was low. "Anything to do with Christmas is that bad."

His words startled like gunshots fired through a silent night. The true depth of his dislike of the holidays struck her with guilt that she'd teased him. Yes, she'd heard him say he didn't like Christmas, had seen his discomfort, but she hadn't truly appreciated how deep his dislike ran, hadn't fully appreciated that he repeatedly set that dislike aside to help her with holiday projects.

"Why?" Why didn't he like Christmas? Why was he willing to set aside that dislike for her? Even before they'd known she was pregnant, he'd played Santa. Because she'd asked him to. He'd also volunteered to help her at the food bank. Because he'd thought she was ill and needed his help.

Looking at him, his handsome face clouded, his eyes full of pain as he stared at the ceramic village, she wavered between reminding herself to protect her heart and risking his rejection by wrapping her arms around him. But she only held on to his arm.

"I don't like Christmas."

If she understood, maybe she could understand him, could understand why he insisted on calling them friends. Out of misplaced honor to his deceased wife and daughter?

"Tell me why you don't like Christmas. Please." She squeezed where she held his arm. "I want to understand you and can't fathom why anyone wouldn't love the holidays."

Silence. More silence.

With his free hand, he raked his fingers through his dark hair. His jaw rotated, then clenched. "Sandra and Shelby died on their way to a Christmas sale."

"Oh, God, no," she gasped. She'd known they'd died in a car crash, had known he professed to dislike the holidays. Why hadn't she put two and two together and come up with the right answer about why he didn't like Christmas?

"It was early morning, before dawn," he continued, staring straight ahead, but she suspected he saw nothing, that he was locked away in a different time. A time where he had endured a horrible tragedy. Had hurt in ways Abby couldn't fix with a little Christmas magic.

Her heart bled for him, at the pain still so evident on his face, at the hollowness in his eyes.

"I'd pulled an all-nighter at the hospital, was still there and didn't know she was going to the sale. When they wheeled her in, I couldn't believe it was her, couldn't fathom why she'd be out that early."

"Oh, Dirk." She wasn't sure he heard her. He didn't appear to even be in the same room with her, his mind was so far removed from the present.

"She'd dragged Shelby out at that godforsaken hour so she could go and buy my Christmas gift." Anger cracked his voice. Deep, hoarse anger that chilled Abby to the core.

She clasped his hand, squeezed. "I'm so sorry, Dirk."

"Yeah, me, too." He looked toward her, met her gaze, and possibly saw her, although she still wasn't sure he wasn't too far lost in the past.

"I'd rather have had my wife and daughter than anything any store sold."

"I know you would." Beyond caring about protecting her heart, she moved to where she could wrap her arms around him, hold him close. "Of course, you would."

He remained stiff in her embrace, not relaxing, not making any move to take her into his arms or acknowledge that she held him.

"There was a Christmas tree in the emergency department's office where they put me after… Christmas music played." His face twisted. "I felt as if Christmas mocked me. The best part of my life was being ripped away when the world was celebrating peace, love and happiness. It didn't seem right."

"What happened was an accident. A tragic accident." She reached up, brushed her fingers over his face, smoothing the tension lines at his temples. "But Sandra and Shelby wouldn't have wanted you to be unhappy, to lose the spirit of Christmas, the spirit of life."

He blinked. "You don't know that."

"Your wife was on her way to purchase a gift for you. Not because of whatever that gift was, but because she wanted to buy you something special. That doesn't sound like a woman who would want her husband to be lonely and miserable at the holidays."

But it wasn't just at the holidays, she realized. Dirk had closed off his heart. Permanently.

"As if my family would let me be lonely at the holidays," he snorted.

He'd never mentioned a family. Only Sandra and Shelby. "Your family?"

Why had Dirk mentioned his family? Just because his mother had called repeatedly over the past week wanting to know if he was coming home for Christmas, attempting to change his mind when he repeatedly said no.

Apparently, she'd also put his brother and sister on the task as well, as both had been using various technologies to insist he come home so the family could all be together for the holidays.

As if he'd want to set himself up for another

miserable confrontation. As if he'd want to give them the opportunity to force him down memory lane with photos and movies like they had the year before until he'd had enough and walked out.

A Christmas intervention. Who ever heard of anything so foolish? Anything so humiliating and embarrassing? Anything so hurtful? He'd been emotionally ambushed and, no matter how well intentioned, they'd ripped away what little balm he'd coated his raw heart with.

They just didn't understand the ache inside him.

No one did.

How could they when they still lived inside their safe little world? Sure, they'd mourned Sandra and Shelby, but they'd moved on, forgotten. Only his mother seemed to have some understanding. She put up Christmas ornaments in honor of Shelby. A baby's first Christmas ornament that had his precious little girl's photo inside.

As much as he wanted his mother to keep

Shelby's memory alive, being surrounded by family only brought home just how much he'd once had. How much he'd lost.

Why had he brought up this subject? He didn't talk about Sandra and Shelby. Neither did he discuss why he didn't like Christmas. Not with anyone. Ever.

He'd never told anyone the details of his wife and daughter's deaths. His family knew, of course. Sandra's sister had shared that they'd planned to meet early at the department store. So early another car had crashed into her head-on when the driver had fallen asleep behind the wheel. A driver who'd also been on her way to an early-morning Christmas sale. All for a few sale-priced items that the recipient hadn't needed to begin with.

If Christmas never came again, Dirk wouldn't care, would be glad to not have to face all the reminders, would be glad not to have his family put so much pressure on him to "live life." What did they think he was doing?

"Dirk?" Abby touched his face, pulling him

to the present. Her palm was warm against his face. "Do you have a large family?"

Closing his eyes, trying to focus on the present, he sighed. "Huge."

When he opened his eyes, Abby's had widened with delight. "Really?"

His stomach ached. "Unfortunately, yes."

She blinked, clearly confused. "Unfortunately?"

"Obviously you've never had a big family."

Looking a little sad, she shook her head. "No, my parents were both only children of older parents. I sort of remember my grandmother, but she died when I was five and the others had passed before her. When my parents died, I went to live with my great-aunt. She died while I was in college. I always wanted a big family."

Dirk studied her, a woman who had no family, had lost a great deal, and thought of what a bright light she was to those who knew her. "How is it you remain so positive when you've had so much loss in your life?"

"Everyone faces loss, although certainly there

are varying degrees. Attitude is a choice and I choose to be happy."

"Even though you're pregnant with my baby?" He hadn't meant his question to sound so negative. Neither had he meant to hold his breath while he waited for her answer.

A smile softened her expression. "This baby is a blessing. I might not have thought so when I first found out, but that was foolishness. Our baby is a miraculous gift. All babies are."

He let out the breath, relaxing a bit that their baby would be loved, that Abby would be able to wrap this baby in her goodness, that she'd make up for the hole where his heart used to be. "You're the gift, Abby."

Clasping his hand, she lifted it to her lips, pressed a soft kiss to his fingers. "I'm thankful for you, too."

Her eyes glittered with compassion, which usually sent him running for the hills, but there was more in Abby's gaze. So much more.

In her eyes he saw hope. Hope that he could be

what she needed. Hope that was a waste of her goodness since her hope centered around him.

Dirk's apartment stood out in stark contrast to Abby's house. No brightly lit Christmas tree. No wrapped packages. No Christmas spice candles. No garland or bows. Nothing.

For that matter, his apartment was stark when not considering the Christmas season. The bare necessities interlaced with a few high-tech niceties. Nothing warm and inviting.

A sofa. A fully loaded entertainment center worthy of hosting all sporting events. A square coffee table with a few sporting and medicine magazines tossed onto it. The area of the room meant to hold a dining table held a weight bench and an elliptical stair machine instead. Two stools sat in front of the bar that divided the kitchen from the open floor plan. The kitchen looked just as barren as the rest of the apartment. As if he barely lived here.

He'd been here, what? Two? Three months? Not a real long time, but enough that a home should begin to reflect its owner. Perhaps this bare one did.

Glancing toward her, Dirk paused, obviously reading her expression. "It's a place to live, Abby."

She nodded, aching more for him than she had since the morning he'd told her about his wife and daughter's deaths. Emotionally, she'd continued to waver back and forth between her growing feelings for Dirk and the pending sense that she needed to ship her heart to the North Pole in the hope of keeping it out of Dirk's clutches.

"It's a nice building."

He threw his head back in laughter. "Which is your way of telling me my apartment is sadly lacking."

Glancing around the sparse rooms again, she shrugged. "Well, at least I know what to get you for Christmas."

Christmas was Tuesday, just a few short days away, and she'd not bought him anything, hadn't known what to get him. She'd figured she'd make him a tin full of peanut-butter goodies, but she wanted to give him something more.

His laughter faded. "I don't want you to get me anything, Abby."

"I know." She bit her lip. She hadn't meant to say that, hadn't meant to mention Christmas at all.

They'd just stopped by his apartment so he could grab a shower and clean clothes, then he'd promised to take her out for dinner. When she wasn't nauseated, she was starved. Today had been one of those days where she couldn't get enough to eat.

"I mean it, Abby. No presents." Of course, Dirk would say he didn't want anything. She understood that, planned to get him something anyway. After seeing his apartment for the first time today, she had a much better idea of things he could use.

"But—"

"No buts. I'm serious. Do not get me a present. I don't celebrate Christmas."

She didn't say anything. How could she? Dirk

was the most important person in her life. She couldn't not get him a present.

He eyed her as if waiting for her to argue. When she didn't, he gestured toward the entertainment center. "Make yourself at home. Watch whatever you like. There's drinks in the refrigerator. I'll only be a few minutes."

Abby nodded, but rather than sit on the over-sized leather sofa she wandered around the barren room. No pictures hung on the wall. No little knickknacks sat on the coffee table. Anyone could have lived here. But Dirk did.

Her heart ached for him all over again. He really had cut himself off from the world after his wife and daughter had died. If not for work, she wondered if he'd have any contact with others. Until her.

She'd definitely pushed him outside his comfort zone with her Santa requests and numerous volunteer stints.

Now they were going to be parents, which definitely pushed his limits. Dirk needed her. Needed this baby. Maybe he didn't realize just how much but, looking around this apartment, Abby did realize.

A loud ring sounded throughout the room. Abby jumped, looked around and spotted Dirk's house phone.

Should she answer? Probably not.

But as the shrill ringing sounded time and again, she decided whoever was calling must really need to talk to him, could possibly even be the hospital as he wouldn't have heard his cell while in the shower.

"Hello?" she said, hoping she was doing the right thing by answering, but knowing at the moment she was the one outside her comfort zone.

Silence.

"Hello?" she repeated, guilt slamming her as surely as if she'd peeked inside a Christmas package. She should have just let the phone ring.

"I was trying to get in touch with Dirk Kelley," a female voice said, sounding a little uncertain.

Whoever the caller was, she hadn't said Dr. Kelley. She'd said Dirk. Abby's guilt over answering the phone skyrocketed. As did her curiosity and some other green monster taking hold in her chest.

"Um, this is Dirk's number. He's not available at the moment. Could I take a message?"

A woman was calling Dirk. Who was she? Why was she calling? What right did Abby have to answer his phone, to take a message?

Every right, her heart shouted. She was pregnant with his baby, had spent the past several days in his company, working, volunteering, getting to know him, and he her.

Silence, then, "Who is this?"

Just exactly what Abby wanted to know, in reverse. But she bit her tongue. Dirk had had another life in Oak Park. Although they'd talked a lot over the past several days, he'd shared very little of that life with her. Had there been someone special? Someone he'd left behind?

The hurt she'd felt when she'd discovered he'd been married, had had a child, and she hadn't known came back. Why had Dirk revealed so little of his past?

"Abby. I, uh, work with Dr Kelley." Why had she called him Dr. Kelley? "We're friends." Why had she added that last? What she really wanted was to insist on knowing who the caller was and why she was calling Dirk.

"Oh," the woman said, slowly, as if digesting Abby's answer. "That's nice. Where is my son that he can't answer his cell or his home phone?"

Her son? This was Dirk's mother!

"Uh," Abby hedged, her face flaming. "He's in the shower."

"Really? Or is he just trying to avoid me insisting on him coming home for Christmas?"

"Dirk's not planning to come home for Christmas?" Abby couldn't fathom having a family and not wanting to spend the holidays with them. Was he not going home because of her pregnancy? Or because of the past?

"He's volunteered to work on the holidays, hasn't he?"

"He's working on Christmas Eve," she admitted. They both were. "He gets off at seven on Christmas morning."

"I'd hoped…" His mother sighed. "No matter what I'd hoped. I'm going to have to face facts. If he refuses to come home, we'll just have to bring Christmas to him. Tell me, Abby, just what's your relationship with my son and how good are you at planning surprises?"

CHAPTER ELEVEN

ON SATURDAY, December twenty-second, Abby watched Dirk spoon a helping of green beans onto a cheap paper plate held by a rough-looking, unshaven, dirty man wearing multiple layers and carrying a toboggan.

Was he the last person to be served lunch?

They'd fed over two hundred today. Too many people with no homes, no food, no family, no Christmas.

She glanced around the dining area of the shelter. Smiling faces. Lots of smiling faces. And chatter. Being warm and having food in their bellies seemed to have turned up the noise level. Along with gift packages that included several basic amenities, baths were being offered. Several had taken the shelter up on that offer, but most had declined.

"This was a good work."

Surprised at Dirk's comment, she turned to him. "Yes. All the charities I volunteer with are good works."

He met her gaze. "You're a good person, Abby."

Slightly uncomfortable at the intensity in his eyes, she shrugged. "I'm no different than anyone else."

The corner of his mouth hitched up in wry amusement. "You're the most giving woman I've ever met."

Ignoring the depth of his look because she quite simply wasn't sure how to take it, she winked playfully. "Thank you. I try."

"Why is that?"

"Why is what?" She wiped the metallic serving area with a washcloth, more to busy her hands than because of any spilt food.

"Why do you do so much for others?"

Feeling her face go warm, she shrugged. "My parents worked for Second Harvest. Both of them. It's how they met. After they died, a lot of people did a lot of things to help me. I want to do my part to give back."

"And?"

And she didn't want to dig any deeper than that. Didn't want to look beyond the obvious reasons for volunteering. "And so I have."

"Why so focused on Christmas?"

She took in his confused expression. "My fondest memories of my parents all revolve around the holidays."

He nodded as if he understood, but she doubted he did. After all, he still had a family who loved him, a family who craved to spend time with him and celebrate special occasions. A family he held at arm's length despite their continued efforts to be close to him.

"The Santa suit you wore was my father's." She wiggled her fingers inside their plastic serving gloves.

"You mentioned that the day you loaned it to me."

"He played Santa every year for various charity groups." How she cherished memories of seeing her father dressed up, of him scooping her into his arms and telling her he was off to be Santa's helper. Once upon a time she'd believed he really was Santa and just couldn't tell her. The times she and her mother had gone with him had been magical. He'd always made her feel special, loved.

"Good for him," the man who'd also played Santa for her said a bit wryly.

Abby just smiled, continuing her blast from the past. "Every Christmas Eve my father would put the suit on and put out my presents. He didn't know I knew, but the last two years, I snuck up and watched."

"You snuck up?" That brought a smile to Dirk's face. "Okay, so you've not always been on the nice list."

"Of course I have always been on the nice list. No way would I ever be on Santa's naughty list." She gave him an innocent look. "When my father had finished putting out my presents, my mom would offer him the cookies we'd made. My last Christmas with them, he pulled her into his lap on the sofa instead. They laughed and giggled and…kissed."

"So you literally saw your mommy kissing Santa?"

She laughed. "Yes, I literally did. I thought it wonderful how much they loved each other, how much fun they had with Christmas. All I ever wanted was to grow up and be like them."

He didn't say anything for a few moments. "Yet you chose nursing instead of going to work in philanthropy?"

Abby stared at him, amazed at how much he saw. She had always planned to go into philanthropy. "My aunt was a nurse. She convinced me I needed career skills to see me through life. I wasn't sure at first, but once I started school, I loved nursing."

"And the philanthropy?"

"I love that, too. Nursing is philanthropic work in many ways. It makes me feel better inside."

"Because you feel closer to your parents when you're helping others?"

Abby wondered how he'd seen what she'd

rarely acknowledged herself, that volunteering made her feel less alone. Particularly at the holidays, when she'd otherwise be trapped inside her house with nothing to distract her from the loneliness of having no family.

"Yes," she admitted, "I guess it does make me feel as if I still have a connection to them."

"That's why the mad rush at Christmas? Because you want to feel closer to your parents?"

"I, well, I don't know. Possibly." She bit the inside of her lower lip, not wanting to admit the depth of her reasons. "They were wonderful parents. I missed them so much after they were gone."

"How did they die?"

"A house fire. Electrical wiring gone bad, according to the fire report. I was at a schoolfriend's house for the night. Everything was destroyed except a few storage bins in the basement." She gave him a blurry-eyed smile. "Those bins had Christmas decorations in them."

His expression softened. "The decorations you have up in your house?"

She nodded, surprised that he'd made the connection, then mentally scolded herself. Of course Dirk would make the connection. The man was brilliant.

"I've added a few pieces over the years, especially to the Christmas village as it's my favorite, and I've had to repair things, but, yes, my decorations are mostly all items that were part of my childhood. The only tangible parts left, actually."

Which explained a lot about Abby's love of Christmas. Dirk sighed, glanced up to see a latecomer standing in the food line, and forced a smile at the unkempt man.

"Green beans?" he asked the man, who was of indeterminate age. Could have been in his forties, could have been in his seventies. A lot of the homeless were like that. They lived such a rough life with exposure to the elements aging them more rapidly and were so rumpled that it was impossible to estimate an accurate age.

The man nodded, extending his plate. Dirk

scooped a big spoonful onto the plate, which was already burgeoning with food.

"Roll?" Abby held one out with her tongs.

Again, the man flashed a toothless grin. "Thanks, pretty girl."

Abby blushed. "You're welcome."

"He's right, you know," Dirk commented when the man walked over to a vacant seat at a half-occupied table. "You are a pretty girl."

"Thanks." But rather than smile at him, as he'd expected, she averted her gaze, wiping at the counter again as if she wasn't quite sure how to take his compliment.

He understood. He didn't know quite how to take his compliment either. Wasn't he the one insisting that they were just friends? Yet he fought the desire to take her into his arms constantly.

She was right to be wary. He didn't want to hurt her, battled with the need to put distance between them.

But she was pregnant with his baby and he couldn't turn his back on her. Wouldn't even if he could.

Soon decisions would have to be made. Decisions Dirk wasn't sure he was ready to make, but he had little choice given the circumstances.

Abby had cooked most of the previous day while Dirk had been at work at the hospital. She'd only had to do last-minute items that simply couldn't be done ahead of time for dinner to taste right.

He should be arriving any moment. Would he be upset with her? He had no idea what she had planned, just that he was coming over for dinner.

Nervously, she swept her gaze around her living room. The tree blinked in multicolored magic. Her village houses glowed invitingly, making Abby imagine strolling along between them, hand in hand with Dirk as they peeped into shop windows and snuggled together to stay warm.

Despite being on edge, she smiled at the memories attached to each one of the special pieces to her mother's Christmas village. She ran her hands over the church's steeple. The first piece her father had given to her mother because it had reminded him of the small church where they'd married.

Mistletoe was in his basket next to her lit fire. Candles burned on the mantel and coffee table, blending with the pine of her tree to add a spicy Christmas scent to the room. Dinner and company waited in the kitchen.

God, she hoped everything went as planned, that his mother hadn't been wrong. But deep in her heart Abby wondered if she'd made a mistake in going along with this Christmas surprise. What if Dirk was upset? What if he thought she'd overstepped her boundaries?

Which was the crux of the matter. What were the boundaries of their relationship? He kept insisting they were just friends, yet he looked at her with desire in his eyes, looked at her with possessiveness in his eyes. She was pregnant with his child, crazily in love with him, and wanted to share her life, their baby's life, with him. But the him she saw, not the broken man he saw reflected in his mirror. She deserved better than walking on emotional eggshells for the rest of their lives.

On cue, the doorbell rang, causing Mistletoe's eyes to open. He yawned, but didn't budge from his basket.

"Nothing fazes you, does it, big guy?" she said to the lazy cat as she walked into the foyer. Pasting a nervous smile on her face, she opened the front door.

A freshly shaven and showered Dirk stood there, looking more handsome than she'd ever seen. Perhaps because he was smiling and running his gaze up and down her.

He held up a bottle. "I'd have brought wine but I figured apple cider was more appropriate considering."

"Um, apple cider is fine." Casting a wary glance over her shoulder toward the kitchen, she motioned him inside, closing the door behind him to block out the cold air rushing in. It hadn't started snowing yet but the weather forecast predicted there was a good chance of it.

Abby took the bottle. "I'll just put this in the kitchen while you remove your coat."

Slipping his coat off, he glanced around the room. "Wow, you've really gone to a lot of trouble for just the two of us."

"About that…" She waited until his eyes connected with hers, trepidation bubbling in her belly.

Only his gaze shot past her to where he could see into the small dining area, could see the table set with eight place settings. His smile faded. "It's not going to be just the two of us? Did you invite some of your friends from the hospital?"

She shook her head. "No, I have a Christmas surprise for you."

Furrows dug into his forehead. "You know how I feel about Christmas."

"I do know." *Please don't let him be upset that she'd gone along with his mother's suggestion. Please.*

"Okay." He exhaled slowly, moving close to her, close enough to touch. "I'm trying to deal with your Christmas excitement, but no more surprises."

Cupping his handsome face, she stared into his eyes, knowing she loved him, knowing she wanted him for ever, to spend all her Christmases with him and their child, and any future children that might come along. "Dirk, I—"

"Dirk! You're here!"

His expression instantly transformed to terseness, instantly tightened with cold accusation before turning toward the woman who'd entered the room.

What the—? Dirk rotated his jaw, counted to ten, inhaled and exhaled, anything to try to keep his mounting anger under control.

"Hello, Mother." He'd never mentioned Abby to his family, so his mother couldn't have been the one to make contact. But how? Surely Abby wouldn't have gone behind his back? This would explain why his mother's calls had eased.

Clearly having no clue as to the enormity of

what she'd done, Abby's fingers clasped his arm. "Dirk?"

Seeing the stricken look in her eyes, he fought the need to reassure her. How could he reassure her when panic gripped his throat, cutting off his airways?

"I'm surprised to see you here, Mother."

She walked to him, turned her cheek up to him. Automatically, he bent to kiss her in spite of his displeasure at her invading his holidays. God, he wasn't up for Christmas Intervention II.

"I can see why you like Philadelphia so much." His mother beamed in Abby's direction. "Your Abby is quite lovely."

"She's not my Abby." But she was quite pale, looking back and forth between them, clearly trying to size up the dynamics taking place. How could she have done this?

"Are the rest of the crew here?" But he could hear that they were. Over the sounds of the Christmas music playing, he could hear his nephews chatting back and forth, hear his sister shushing them.

"Holidays are meant to be shared with your family. We wanted to spend ours with you, Dirk, because we love you."

He raked his fingers through his hair. "So you invited yourself to Abby's?"

"No," his mother laughed, wrapping her arms around him to give him a hug. "I mentioned how much we wanted to see you over the holidays, that we planned to surprise you with a visit, and asked your lovely Abby to help. She invited us here. Such a good girl, Dirk. I like her."

Dirk struggled to process his mother's words. "When did you talk to Abby?"

His mother gave him one last squeeze, starting to look a little nervous herself. "We've talked several times over the past week. She's absolutely lovely, son."

"Yes, you've mentioned that a time or two," he bit out tersely. God, what were they up to? If they brought out video tapes and photo albums again, he was out of there.

"I'll, uh, I'll go check on dinner." Abby gave him one last look, her lower lip trembled, then she disappeared into the kitchen, the low rumble of his brother's voice greeting her.

Abby had had no right to invite his family, to plan a Christmas dinner with them behind his back. Just what had his family told her? That he was a broken man? Pathetic and weak at the loss of his wife and child? That he might as well have died in that car wreck, too?

He should have. Sandra and Shelby should have lived. He should have been the one taken that morning.

"Dirk." His mother gave him a look that would have stopped him in his tracks during his younger years. "When I spoke with Abby, I'd hoped Philadelphia had been good for you, had removed the blinkers you've worn for the last four years. It's time you dealt with this."

Something inside Dirk snapped.

"Have you ever considered that I have dealt with this, only not to everyone else's satisfaction? Guess what, Mother, I'm the one who has to wake up every single day knowing that I will never look into my wife's eyes again, that I will never feel Shelby's fingers wrapped around mine again. You should respect that I've dealt with this and let me be."

"If you'd dealt with this, we wouldn't be having this conversation, would we? Because you would have come home for Christmas."

"What? And be put through the hell of last year? I don't think so."

"We hired a top psychiatrist, Dirk. We followed her recommendations to the letter—"

"A psychiatrist?" Oh, God, that was rich. "I'm not crazy."

"No one thinks you are."

He paced across the room, spun to meet her gaze. "I was ambushed last Christmas."

She took a deep breath and didn't back down. "You were surrounded by people who love you and want what's best for you. People who want you to enjoy life again."

"What was best for me is lying in a cemetery in Oak Park." Dirk couldn't stop the words from streaming out of his mouth. Couldn't stop the feelings of hurt and betrayal streaming through him. "Something you conveniently forgot when you planned last year's fiasco. Tell me, what Christmas torture do you have in store for me tonight? Pictures? Home movies? Personal rec-ollections of my wife and daughter? Because if that's the case, you should leave now, and take the rest of the family with you."

A loud gasp caused both Dirk and his mother to spin toward the kitchen door. Abby held on to the door frame as if she might slide to the floor if she didn't.

Sharp pain zig-zagged across her face.

Hell. He raked his fingers through his hair. What was wrong with him? He'd never verbally attacked his mother before. Not even last year during the worst of the intervention, right before he'd walked out on them. No, he'd just calmly gotten up, informed them that they were mis-taken about him and that he was leaving. And he'd left.

His mother recovered before he did, pasting a weak smile to her face as she regarded Abby. "I'm sorry, dear. It's rude of us to come into your house and squabble over family disagreements."

Family disagreements? Dirk wanted to laugh. Was that what they were calling invading his life?

"I came to tell you dinner was finished if you're ready to eat." Disillusionment shone on her face and when their eyes met, she quickly averted her gaze from his.

"Dinner would be lovely." His mother took him by the elbow, gave him a look meant to put him in his place. "Everything smells wonderful. Right, son?"

Dirk gritted his teeth, seeing right through his mother's ploy. She wanted to pretend everything was okay for Abby's sake. If they'd cared about him, or Abby, they'd have stayed in Oak Park, wouldn't have come to stir up the past.

"Right," he finally agreed, knowing this was going to be a long, long night.

* * *

Abby's face hurt from keeping her fake smile in place, just as she'd kept her smile in place all evening.

"It was so lovely to meet you, dear." Dirk's mother leaned forward, engulfing Abby in a giant bear hug. One so real and heartfelt Abby wanted to cry. "At least we know Dirk has someone to look out for him here in Philly."

Right. But during the terse evening Abby had realized she didn't want to look out for Dirk. Not under the current circumstances.

Having watched him with his family had only made obvious what she'd admitted to herself weeks ago but had shoved aside, hoping that Dirk could love her. He couldn't. He had closed off his heart to the world.

If he wasn't willing to let his own mother in, how was Abby supposed to believe he'd ever let her?

Which was the crux of the matter. After tonight, she didn't believe.

Dirk had stolen her belief in happily-ever-after, her belief in Christmas miracles. Her belief, period.

In place of the hope-filled woman she'd once been was a disillusioned woman but one determined to be strong woman who'd do what was best for her child.

"Dinner was lovely," said the next woman in line to head out the front door. A tall, dark-haired woman with eyes identical to Dirk's. His sister, Jolene. She held a well-bundled toddler in her arms. A toddler who shared the Kelley eyes. Would Abby's own baby have a similar blue gaze? Would she forever be haunted by the man she'd loved but who hadn't been able to love her in return?

"Thanks so much for inviting us." The woman leaned over and kissed Abby's cheek. "I hope to see you again soon. Maybe Dirk will bring you to Oak Park."

Abby felt tears pop into her eyes. What kind of man could have a family like this and shut them out?

Oh, he'd lightened up a bit as the evening had

progressed, but he'd been out-and-out rude when he'd first arrived. So much so that Abby had planted the fake smile on her face and tried to make his family feel welcome despite his cold regard. Even now, as his mother pulled him into her arms, he wore a slight grimace, stood stiffly rather than embracing her in return.

Abby wanted to hit him. He had this beautiful family, her baby's family, and he ignored them, held them at arm's length.

No doubt after his wife and daughter's deaths things had been rough, but shouldn't he have leaned on his family, not shut them out?

His brother shook his hand, pulled him into a half-embrace. "Good to see you, man. If you can swing it, we'd love to have you at Christmas."

Dirk didn't comment. By his brother's sigh, Abby figured John knew Dirk had no intention of showing up in Oak Park on Christmas Day.

"He'll probably sleep most of the day. After all, he'll have just pulled twenty-four hours in the emergency room." Why was she defending him? This was his family. Not hers. She shouldn't be the one working so hard to make things go smoothly. "Driving long distances after working such a long shift really wouldn't be wise."

"You're right, of course." His mother's chest rose and fell beneath her heavy coat. "At least he won't be spending Christmas alone." She sent Abby a warm smile. "It really was lovely to meet you. Come on, children. Let's get this show on the road so Abby can prop her feet up. She looks tired."

Something in the way Dirk's mother said the words made Abby meet the woman's gaze, made her look away because she was sure the woman could see into her soul and see all her secrets.

Besides, she *was* tired. After pulling a twelve-hour shift at the hospital, coming home and grabbing only a few hours' sleep then finishing dinner, she was tuckered out.

It took Dirk's family another five minutes to completely get out the door, between more good-byes, hugs, kisses to the cheeks, and kids dashing back in for a cookie for the road.

When the door closed, Abby sagged and didn't

bother to try to hide her fatigue from Dirk. As his family had exited, she'd sensed his mounting tension, had seen the building fire in his eyes, had known they'd argue and was ready to get it over with.

"How could you treat your family that way, Dirk? They love you, drove all that way to spend the evening with you, and you lashed out at them every chance you got." Her heart had ached for the whole lot of them. Even Dirk. Because in his grief he'd lost much more than his wife and daughter. He'd lost everything that mattered and had no one to blame but himself.

"They had no right to show up here. How could you have invited them without discussing it with me first?"

"This is my house. I can invite whomever I want," she reminded him, chin lifting a notch. "Besides, your mother wanted to surprise you. I thought you'd be happy to see your family over the holidays."

"Well, I wasn't. You want to know why? Because I'm not you. I'm not little Miss Christmas Spirit, spreading good tidings to the whole world. I'm a man who lost his wife and daughter and the world, including his family who should under-stand, expects him to go on and forget."

"You weren't the only one who lost someone they loved when Shelby and Sandra died. Your family loved them, too."

"You have no idea what you're talking about," he scoffed.

"Whose fault is that, Dirk? I'm pregnant with your baby and yet you'd never introduced me to your family. Even tonight, you acted as if I was no one special."

"How did you want me to act? You went behind my back."

"It was supposed to be a pleasant surprise! Something to give you good memories to replace the ones you refuse to let go of."

"You'd have me forget my wife and daughter?" His eyes blazed, the veins on his neck bulged, his breath hissed.

Needing to put distance between them, Abby turned away, walked over to her Christmas village table, hoping to find comfort in the heirlooms she loved.

"Answer me." Dirk followed her, gripped her arm, turned her toward his angry face. "Is that what this was about? Making me forget Sandra and Shelby for your own purposes? Being pregnant doesn't give you the right to go behind my back, Abby."

"My only purpose was to give you a special Christmas memory, which you ruined for everyone by closing yourself off to any possibility of having a good time."

"I have all the special Christmas memories I need."

"Well, good for you, Dirk," she bit out, tired, frustrated, hurt, angry at him for his callous attitude. "Maybe you should stop to think about everyone else who might still want new special Christmas memories instead of being such a selfish jerk!"

She jerked back, freeing herself from his grasp and losing her balance. She stumbled, reached out to steady herself. And failed.

CHAPTER TWELVE

IN HORRID slow motion Dirk watched disaster unfold, unable to stop what had been set into play, only able to do damage control by reacting quickly.

Reaching out to keep from falling back, Abby had grabbed hold of the table her village sat on. Only she didn't catch the table. She caught the steeple of the church and kept going, the church traveling with her, knocking pieces of the village left and right.

"No," she cried as she kept going back, too off balance to do a thing to stop the pending catastrophe as the table tipped. "My mother's village!"

But rather than saving her houses, Dirk caught hold of her, righting her while the table and its contents crashed to the floor.

The sound of glass crashing into glass sent her cat tearing from the room with a screech.

"Are you okay?" he asked, visually checking her, grateful not to see any blood as she could easily have cut herself on the broken pieces.

"My mother's village!" She pulled free of him and dropped to her knees, picking up the pieces.

"Those are just things. Are you okay? The baby?"

When he'd watched her falling back, his anger had dissipated into fear. Fear that she might be hurt, that she might lose the baby.

Abby ignored his questions about her well-being and righted the table. She picked up the church first, noted the missing steeple, the chip at the base. She dug her fingernail into the chipped area and took a deep breath, then continued to pick up piece after piece.

Dirk knew that she connected the decorations with her family, with the connection the three of them had once shared.

He bent to help her, picking up the pieces of the

train set and placing them back on the righted table, carefully reconnecting the track, the train engine and cars. Two of the houses were intact, so was the schoolhouse. The carousel had a tiny chip at the base. All the other village houses had larger breaks.

Dirk took her hands into his. "Sit down, Abby. This is only upsetting you. I'll do the rest, save what can be salvaged."

"No. I think you've already done enough, don't you?" Her chin lifted. Her eyes blazed, blazed so intently that Dirk winced. He'd never seen that anguish, that pain, that accusation in Abby's eyes before.

"I didn't do this, Abby." But he hadn't been innocent. He'd been so wrapped up in his own emotions over his family's "surprise" that he hadn't considered Abby's emotions, hadn't acknowledged that she'd been trying to do something good by having his family there. Instead, he'd attacked the moment they'd walked out the door.

"No, I did this," she admitted, glaring at him. "I ruined my mother's Christmas village."

A coldness had crept into Abby's voice. A coldness he'd never heard from her. A coldness that held finality.

Her fingers clasped tightly the church steeple she held. She looked ready to snap into as many pieces as the village collection had.

She looked like she wanted to snap him into a zillion pieces and toss him out with the trash.

Abby didn't say anything more. She couldn't. Her throat had swollen shut with emotion. Her voice gone. Perhaps for ever.

She stared at the church's steeple in her shaking hands. Her entire insides shook. Her mother's Christmas village. Broken.

How could she have been so stupid as to fall into the table? How could she have been so stupid as to fall in love with a man who could never love her back?

"Abby?"

She sucked in a breath, knowing she couldn't

just keep sitting here, staring at the shattered remains of the only tangible things she had of happier times, of her childhood.

The damage was done. There was no undoing it. She'd make do with the best she could, to repair the pieces she could repair. Try not to wonder if fate wasn't trying to tell her something.

That she might dream of the wonderful Christmas village scenario with Dirk, but all she was going to get was shattered dreams, and the sooner she accepted that, the less she'd have her hopes crushed.

"These are just things. You still have your memories of the Christmases with your parents. That's what's important."

Hearing Dirk say that made something snap inside Abby. Something that perhaps had been on edge from the moment she'd found out she was pregnant. From the moment she'd realized she'd never have her happily-ever-after dream. Never have magical Christmases of her own. Never have what her parents had had. Tonight, watching him with his family, had shattered all hope.

"How dare you call my mother's Christmas village 'things'?" she accused. "You, the man who could care less about his family."

"I care about my family."

She rolled her eyes at him. "You have an odd way of showing it."

"You don't understand my relationship with my family."

"Your family doesn't understand your relationship with them. Nor do they like it. God, you are so lucky to have a family to love you, but you know what? You don't deserve them, Dirk."

His jaw worked as he regarded her. "My relationship with my family is none of your business."

Unable to sit still another moment, she stood, glared down at him. "You're right. It's not. I'm just pregnant you're your child. A fact you haven't bothered to share with your family."

He stood, did some glaring of his own. "I thought you didn't want anyone to know."

"Great excuse, but we're not talking about anyone. We're talking about your family. Our baby's family." She'd never wanted to shake another human being before, but at that moment she wanted to shake Dirk. To jar some sense into him. "Are you embarrassed by me? Or were you not planning on telling them about me ever?"

Oh, God. Was that what the problem had been tonight? Dirk hadn't wanted his family to know about her? Hadn't wanted them to know he'd knocked up some naive nurse who'd fallen in love with him at first sight? Oh, God. She had fallen in love at first sight. Just as her parents had. Only Dirk hadn't fallen in love with her. He didn't even want his family to know she existed, had been a jerk because she'd invited them for Christmas dinner.

"It's not like that." He looked as if he'd like to wrap his fingers around her and do some shaking of his own.

"They don't understand how I feel. No one does."

Which said it all. Said exactly where she fit

into the grand scheme of things. She'd given and given to him. Of her time and her heart. And although Dirk had given of his time, had helped her at her volunteer stints, he hadn't given her of his heart. Not once.

"Maybe it's because you keep your heart locked up inside and won't let anyone close, including your family."

"You don't know what you're talking about."

Abby just stared at him.

His look of annoyance grew. "You have no idea how much trouble you've caused me by inviting them here."

Trouble as in they'd be asking about her?

"Well, I'm sorry to inconvenience you."

His jaw clenched, and he exhaled slowly. "Quit misreading everything I say."

"Or maybe, for the first time, I'm reading everything the right way," she said, knowing in her heart that it was true. She'd believed in Dirk's inner goodness. Had even believed that he'd come around regarding Christmas.

She really had been naive.

If not for her pregnancy, Dirk wouldn't be there. It was only his sense of responsibility that kept him coming round. Which wasn't nearly enough to base a future on.

Not nearly enough for her heart.

Abby longed to sob at her loss, but she wouldn't cry in front of him, wouldn't let him see how much she hurt. Instead, she turned her back toward him and went to the sofa and collapsed onto the plush upholstery.

"Leave, Dirk. I don't want you here." She hadn't known she was going to say the words, but once they left her lips she knew they were right, the only words she could say. Just like the Christmas village, her dreams, any hope of a future between them was shattered.

Silent, he walked over and sat down on the opposite end of the sofa. "You don't want me to go."

She gawked at his audacity. "Actually, I do. I saw a side of you tonight I never want to see again. You have no idea how lucky you are to have those people. They love you and want to be a part of your life."

"They are a part of my life."

"On the periphery perhaps."

"I've already told you, I talk to them routinely."

"About what? The weather? Sports? What is it you talk to them about? Because I got the impression they didn't know quite what to say to you tonight."

"There were no conversational lulls."

"No, there weren't, but no thanks to you."

"I warned you that I wasn't big on company."

"Family is not the same thing as company. Family is everything." But not to Dirk. He'd lost the only family that mattered to him, couldn't see what was within his reach. And Abby had had enough. More than enough. She leapt from her sofa, flung open her front door. "Get out of my house, Dirk."

"Abby—"

"Leave!" she shouted. "And don't ever bother me again."

Without another word, he gave her one last angry look, then left.

Abby started a hep lock while Dirk shined a light into their patient's eyes.

Since he'd left her house the night before, she'd been fighting melancholy. She'd hoped he'd say he wanted to change, that he wouldn't leave, that he planned to spend Christmas Day with her. Every day with her for the rest of his life. But she'd known better.

With as much time as they'd spent together over the last week, she'd thought she wouldn't be alone this Christmas, had believed deep in her heart that she'd spend the day with Dirk. How could she have been so foolish as to get her hopes up? Her hopes had been higher than the North Pole.

What would Dirk do today? Sleep? Flip through television channels? Pretend it was no different from any other day of the year? He wouldn't be driving to his mother's for Christmas, wouldn't be embracing the wonderful family she envied. More the pity for him.

But that wasn't her problem. Not any more. She'd meant what she'd told him. She didn't want him in her life. Not when he refused to acknowledge that what they'd shared had been more than friendship. Not when he refused to open his heart to love again. To open his heart to his family.

Which was why she'd ignored his phone calls today. Why she'd ignored his attempts to talk to her tonight. What was left to be said between them?

She loved Christmas.

He hated Christmas.

She loved family.

He'd shut his out.

Could they be any further apart? She didn't think so.

"How did you fall?" Dirk asked the patient, pulling Abby back to the present. She bit the inside of her lip. She had to stay focused just a little while longer. Her shift was almost at an end. She could do this. Would do this. Then she'd talk to the nurse supervisor about having her schedule changed, changed to dates when she wouldn't have to work with Dirk.

"My wife was complaining about the angle of the star on top of the Christmas tree. I climbed a stepladder, and it tipped."

Dirk's lips compressed into a tight line. Clearly, he blamed Christmas for the man's tragedy. Was it easier for him to blame the holidays than to accept that accidents happened? He'd sure been quick enough to point out that accidents occurred when it had been her village pieces involved.

Village pieces that she'd painstakingly spent the day trying to glue back together.

"Do you recall how you landed? What you hit? How your weight was distributed?"

"It happened kind of fast, Doc." The man scratched his head with the hand Abby didn't have stabilized. "I know I hit my head." The pump knot on his forehead attested to that. "And my right ribs are sore."

"This happened about eight last night?"

The man nodded.

"What made you decide to come to the hospital this morning?"

"I woke up and couldn't breathe. I think that's what woke me."

"Are you still short of breath?"

The man nodded. "Not as badly as at the house. My wife says I had a panic attack."

"Your oxygen saturation is ninety-two percent. That's not too bad," Dirk explained. "But it's not as high as it should be in an otherwise healthy person either. I'm going to order a few tests just to check you out and make sure you haven't fractured any ribs or worse."

"Worse?"

"Fall injuries can result in serious damage to a person's body."

The man nodded. "Tell me something I don't know."

As always, Dirk responded to his patient, making Abby wonder how he could smile so sincerely at a virtual stranger and not his own kin. "Maybe you should stay off ladders for a while, too. Ask someone to help you with anything that requires climbing."

"Tell that to my wife. She has no patience and had to have that star straightened before the kids and grandkids show up in the morning for Christmas celebrations."

Finishing what she was doing, Abby excused herself and disappeared out of the bay.

The moment she finished giving report, she rushed away, determined to somehow find joy in the most magical day of the year.

Her favorite day of the year.

His least favorite day of the year.

A day she'd spend alone yet again.

Christmas Eve shouldn't be a busy night in the emergency room, but this one was. Midnight had come and gone, so technically Christmas morning had arrived.

The only thing Dirk liked about Christmas was it meant the end was near. The end of the season, the decorations, the smells, the aggravation and harassment from family.

Yes, the signal that the end of the season was near was the best part of Christmas Day.

Or it had been.

Now he wasn't so sure. Somehow he'd tangled thoughts of Abby up with Christmas and the thought of the end put his insides in a viselike grip.

The end of Christmas. The end of his relationship with Abby. No, he wouldn't accept that. Not under the circumstances.

God, his family would be ecstatic when they found out she was pregnant. How many times had they attempted to set him up with someone when he'd lived in Oak Park? How many times had they told him to find someone new and start over? How many times had they called to say how much they'd liked Abby, what a great cook she was, what a warm house she'd had, what a generous person she'd seemed? And he'd let them, because Abby's accusations had kept playing over and over in his head.

None of his family had understood that he

hadn't wanted a new start, that he'd wanted his old life, a life that had been snatched away.

A life that had ended on the day his wife and daughter had died. Dirk had buried himself right along with them.

He hadn't been happy in years. Hadn't even really wanted to be. He'd preferred to wallow in his grief.

Until Abby.

In moving away, he had started over.

Quite frankly, that had scared the hell out of him. Had put him on the defensive. Had caused mixed emotions to surge. Emotions that made him want to cling to Abby and the hope she gave him. Emotions that made him want to pack up his bags and get out of Dodge. Emotions that had made him hold her at arm's length, just as she'd nailed him for doing to his family.

But he and Abby had a baby on the way.

A baby.

A precious new life that he and Abby had made.

When she'd fallen into her Christmas village

table, he'd only been able to think of her safety, their baby's safety. Maybe he could have righted the table had he gone for it instead, but all he'd been concerned about had been keeping Abby from falling to the floor.

Because he wanted to keep her safe. Wanted to keep their baby safe.

He'd left when she'd asked him to, seeing she had been too upset to have the talk they needed to have, sensing that the emotions of both of them had been running too high. He'd been fine on his drive home. Fine when he'd walked through the front door. But when he'd crawled into his bed, alone, he'd done what he hadn't done in years. Not since right after Sandra and Shelby's accident. He'd been fairly positive there were no tears left inside him. The night the woman and her daughter died in the E.R. had been his first clue he might be wrong. He'd felt a crack in the protective wall that guarded his heart. Making love with Abby had sent a whole lot of bricks tumbling to the ground. Bricks he'd needed to keep himself safe.

But with Abby, she came first. Her and their baby. In that, she'd bulldozed right through the barriers around his heart, leaving him vulnerable.

Leaving him exposed to her warmth. Exposed to needing her. He'd been fighting to keep from making love to her every second they were together but as much as he'd enjoyed the passion they'd shared, he hadn't enjoyed how much he'd needed her, how connected he'd felt to her, how much he'd hurt if something happened to Abby.

She'd been right about him. He had kept his family at a distance. Had kept them at arm's length. How could he not? He'd always been the strong one in the family, but after Sandra and Shelby's deaths, he hadn't been strong.

He'd hated them seeing him that way.

Hated anyone seeing him that way.

So he'd shut them out.

No wonder they'd held an intervention.

He'd needed one. And more.

He'd needed Abby, so much so that he'd tried

to hold her at arm's length, too, for fear of loving again, of possibly losing that love again.

Need had won out. Need and so much more.

He loved Abby. And wanted to risk holding her and the baby they'd made close to his heart.

But judging by the way she hadn't returned his calls, had all but ignored him since her arrival at shift change, he might have realized too late.

God, he couldn't lose Abby. In her, he'd found his salvation. Had found himself again.

If he'd lost her, he had no one to blame except himself. But he refused to accept that she wouldn't forgive his ignorance.

It was Christmas. A day of miracles. A day meant to be with the ones you loved. Somehow, he'd show Abby he could be the man she and their child needed.

A man who could be whole and start living again.

A man he desperately wanted to be.

Abby's man.

If he had to go to drastic measures to make that happen, then so be it.

CHAPTER THIRTEEN

IF EVER Abby would forgive him, this had to be the way. Hell, he hoped he wasn't wrong. Otherwise he was going to look like the biggest idiot who'd ever walked the face of the earth.

Which didn't bother him near as much as the thought of not winning Abby's forgiveness, of winning her love and trust.

It had taken him several hours to make arrangements for what he wanted to do.

But, finally, here he stood. Most likely she'd already gone to bed, would sleep for several hours.

Maybe it was wrong of him, but Dirk helped himself to the hide-a-key she'd told him where to find on the day he'd knocked and knocked without her answering.

Her house was quiet. Just as he'd expected it to be.

Not even Mistletoe was anywhere to be seen.

Quietly, closing the front door behind him, Dirk set into play what he hoped would show Abby everything in his heart.

"Meow."

Abby groaned, rubbed her face at where a paw swatted at her. "Go back to sleep, Mistletoe. Didn't you get the memo? I'm going to sleep through Christmas this year."

"Meow." Another swat at her face.

Abby rolled onto her side, pulled her pillow over her head, hoping to gain a few more minutes of sleep before having to get up and face the reality of another Christmas spent alone.

That's when she heard another noise.

What was that? Music? Singing?

She stretched, pushing the pillow away from her head and straining to hear.

Definitely Christmas music.

Coming from somewhere in her house.

She had not left music on.

She knew she hadn't.

Someone was in her house.

Panic squeezed at her throat. Then, climbing out of her bed, she laughed at herself. What? A burglar had broken in and put on Christmas music? Right.

She must still be asleep, be dreaming.

Either that or Dirk had used the hide-a-key and if that was the case, she knew she was dreaming.

Dirk wouldn't be playing Christmas music.

But apparently someone would. Maybe Danielle had taken pity on her and come over to surprise her.

Tiptoeing down the hallway, Abby rubbed her eyes, certain she wasn't seeing clearly. Mixed emotions hit her at the sight of the man arranging Christmas packages under her tree.

The man she'd told to get out and not to come back.

How dared he come into her house and, well, whatever it was he was doing?

"I should have you arrested for breaking and entering."

* * *

At the sound of Abby's voice, Dirk turned from where he worked. Hell, he hadn't finished with what he'd wanted to do.

Still, he'd made great headway.

"Ho. Ho. Ho." Yes, he sounded stupid even to himself, but he had a lot riding on this. He'd seen the look in Abby's eyes, had seen that she'd given up on him. It was going to take a desperate act to win her back. This stunt was about as desperate as desperate got. He wished he'd been able to finish. "You're not supposed to be out of bed yet."

Her glare didn't let up. "You need to leave."

He'd meant to change into her father's Santa suit, had meant to give her the kind of Christmas Day she longed for, one like her parents had shared. "I will, but let me finish what I came to do first."

She crossed her arms over her flannel-pajama-covered chest. She glanced around the room, took in the presents he'd arranged, the Santa suit he had draped across the back of the sofa.

"What are you doing?"

"Delivering presents." Lots and lots of presents. Packages of various shapes and sizes were brightly wrapped and overflowing beneath the tree. It had cost him a small fortune to hire the personal shoppers to find stores open on Christmas morning, but if you were willing to spend enough, a person could do most anything. Even do major Christmas shopping on the great day itself.

"Why would you do that? You don't even like Christmas." She stood in the doorway, staring at him as if she really had caught Dr. Seuss's Grinch stealing her Christmas rather than him in jeans and a T-shirt and a bundle of good intentions.

Obviously, he'd become overzealous when he'd turned on the Christmas tunes, thinking she was tired enough that the low music wouldn't disturb her and she'd sleep a few more hours. He'd just have to go forward as things were and pray for the best, pray for Abby to love him.

"Women aren't the only ones allowed to change their minds. Apparently I just needed to be reminded of the real meaning of the holiday."

"Oh, you needed that all right," she scoffed, eyeing him suspiciously. "So you've supposedly changed your mind about Christmas? Why?"

"You."

"Me?" This time she laughed with a great deal of irony. "I changed your mind about Christmas?"

"You changed my mind about everything, Abby. About life. My life. And the life I want with you."

This had to work. If Christmas magic didn't open Abby's eyes to the man he wanted to be for her, nothing would.

Abby crossed the room, stood next to him, but didn't sit, just stared at him with her forehead creased. "What about Sandra? Shelby? You still love them."

"You'd have me not love them?"

"No," she began hesitantly.

"I realize that part of my life is in the past, Abby. I've accepted that. I'm ready to move on to the future. With you."

She glanced away, closed her eyes. "That's too

bad, Dirk, because I don't trust you with my future."

He winced, but wasn't ready to admit defeat. Not when he was battling for the most important part of his life.

"Someone once told me that Christmas Day was the most magical day of the year. A day when miracles can happen." He prayed some of that Christmas magic would shine on him, would help Abby to see how much he loved her. "Trust me, Abby. I won't let you down. Never again."

She didn't say anything for a few moments then met his gaze warily. "How can I believe you? How can I know this isn't some ploy out of a sense of responsibility because I'm pregnant?"

Dirk's ribs squeezed his lungs. He'd hoped she'd say that she did trust him with her heart. That she wanted him and wanted to be a family with him and their baby.

Instead she looked at him with distrust shining in her hazel eyes. God, he'd been such a fool. How many times had Abby opened up her heart to him and he'd pushed her away out of fear?

Fear of feeling again. Fear of loving and losing that love. Fear of feeling because with feeling came the risk of pain.

But there came a point when a man had to overcome his fears, had to risk that pain, had to risk rejection, because the alternative wasn't acceptable. Regardless of the risk of pain, not telling Abby the truth wasn't acceptable.

He took her hand in his. "You've had me from the moment we met, Abby. I tried fighting it, but I think I fell for you in the E.R. that first night. I know I wanted you in that instance. And every instance since."

Her gaze lowered to their interlocked hands, then lifted back to his. "Why are you saying these things? Why now?"

"Because I can't bear the thought that I might have lost you. Tell me you'll give me a chance to prove to you that I can be the man of your dreams."

A tear trickling down her cheek, she closed her eyes. "I didn't really wake up, did I? I'm still asleep and am dreaming."

Dirk lifted her hand to his lips, pressed a kiss to her fingertips. "Then don't wake up quite yet, because this dream is far from over. You have a lot of presents to open."

As if hearing Dirk say he wanted to be the man of her dreams wasn't enough to convince Abby that she was dreaming, the number of packages under her tree clinched the deal.

Never in her life had she had so many presents.

But why was he doing this?

Sitting on the floor, she picked up a box, shook it prior to carefully unwrapping it to reveal a beautiful aqua-colored baby blanket.

He'd bought a gift for their baby. For her. God, could he be serious about wanting to share a future?

Running her fingers over the soft, fuzzy material, she lifted her gaze to his. "This is beautiful."

He reached for the next present and handed it to her. They repeated the process until she was surrounded with baby items. Some pink. Some blue. Some a mixture of pastels.

"You've been busy," she mused, biting into her lower lip, trying to decipher the meaning behind his gifts.

"I had help, but don't hold that against me." He gave a crooked grin. "Even Santa utilizes elves."

"Ah," she said, not quite believing he'd gone to so much trouble to bring her Christmas alive, to give her a magical day despite the fact they'd argued the last time they'd really talked, that she'd told him to leave. "Thank you, Dirk. I love everything."

She did. Not only because these were the first baby items for their child but because they'd come from Dirk. But what did all this mean? Why was he here? Giving her presents?

"Do you, Abby?"

She lifted her gaze to his in question.

"Love everything, that is?"

Abby's breath caught at the intensity in his

blue eyes. At the vulnerability she saw shining there.

No protective walls. No barriers. No hanging on to the past. Just a man asking if she loved him.

A man who she loved with all her heart, but…

Glancing away when she didn't immediately answer, Dirk scratched his chin. "Um…" His voice broke slightly. "Better let me check my bag. Seems like there might be another present for you."

Abby wanted to stop him, to explain her pause, to ease what had put that break in his voice, but the moment had passed and she wondered if some of those fallen walls had been re-erected.

"You shouldn't have."

"Might not want to shake this one," he warned, causing Abby's curiosity to grow as she took the package.

She unwrapped the present, lifted her gaze to his, and caught her breath at what she saw re-flected in his eyes.

He hadn't re-erected any walls, had left his heart bare for her to see, for her to take if she wanted.

She swallowed, glancing back down at the gift in her hands. "I can't believe you had someone find this for me."

"Actually, I had this one in my truck on Saturday night," he explained. "I'd meant to give it to you after our quiet dinner."

"Only we didn't have a quiet dinner." She pulled the piece from the box, carefully removed the protective wrapping, stared in amazement at the antique village piece. A piece that matched her mother's pieces. How had he known? And that he'd bought it before the crash made it all the more special. He wasn't trying to replace something he felt responsible for breaking. He was giving her something from the heart, giving her something because he'd known it would mean something to her, would make her happy.

"I love it," she whispered, leaning forward to kiss his cheek and hoping he couldn't tell she was choking back tears.

"And I love you, Abby."

She almost dropped the house. "Dirk?"

"I love you, Abby," He repeated words sweeter than any melody. "With all my heart. I didn't think I'd ever love again, that I could ever love. But I do. I love you. And our baby. Please forgive me. I've been such a fool, wasted so much time we could have been together."

Taking a moment to steady her nerves, she put the house back into its box, took a deep breath. "Tell me again."

"I've been a fool—"

"Not that part," she interrupted, meeting his gaze, amazed at the emotion reflected there. "Tell me you love me again, Dirk. Please."

Eyes shining with everything Abby had ever hoped to see in a man's gaze, he took her hand into his, lifted it to his lips. "I love you, Abby. Completely. Always. For ever."

"I love you, too." She wrapped her arms around him, leaned in to kiss him, to show him everything in her heart.

But rather than take her into his arms and kiss

her, he held her hands and stared into her eyes, looking almost nervous as he slid his hands into a jeans pocket and pulled out a small box, snapped it open. "Marry me, Abby."

"What?" An earthquake hit right in the pit of Abby's stomach. One whose aftershocks caused wave after wave of emotion to crash through her.

She stared in awe at the marquis-cut diamond reflecting the multicolored lights from the tree.

"Agree to be my wife. To share your life with me. To share all your Christmases with me. Always."

Abby couldn't believe her ears but, looking into his sincere eyes, she knew he was serious, knew he really did love her. No way would Dirk Kelley be pulling that ring free of its box and slipping it onto the third finger of her left hand otherwise.

She stared down at the ring, at where he held her hand. Could this really be happening?

"What about Sandra? Shelby?" she asked, not

quite able to accept that her dreams might be coming true.

"They'll always be a part of my past, a part of who I am. But you are my future, Abby. You and our baby."

"I would never ask you to forget them, Dirk."

"I know you wouldn't, Abby. That's just one of the many reasons I love you. That and how you see the good in everything, including a man who'd lost track that there was anything good left in him."

"There's so much good in you, Dirk. Anyone who'd ever seen you with a patient would know that." She brushed her fingers across his cheek.

"But only you saw. Only you believed in me when I didn't believe in myself. All I knew was that from the moment we met I felt different, alive for the first time in years. You put breath back into my dying body, Abby. Say you'll let me love you always."

"Yes," she whispered, tears brimming in her eyes. "Oh, yes, Dirk."

This time Dirk took her into his arms, kissed her so thoroughly she'd have sworn she must be wearing that halo made of mistletoe, made love to her so thoroughly she'd swear they rocked the Christmas tree.

"Hey, Abs?" Dirk said much later, holding her against him.

"Hmm?"

A sheepish look shone on his face. "Your house wasn't the only place on Santa's list."

Realization hit her and Abby's heart swelled with love and pride of this wonderful man who'd truly opened his heart. "We're going to your family's for Christmas?"

He nodded. "I've got some making up for the past to do. Especially to my mother."

"What time are we supposed to be there?"

He brushed her hair away from her face, pressed a kiss against her temple. "They don't know we're coming, so whenever we arrive will be okay."

She wrapped her arms around him, kissed the corner of his mouth, excited at the magic filling the day. "Your mother is going to be so happy when you walk through that door, Dirk."

"She's going to be even happier when I tell her our news."

"That we're getting married?"

"That she's getting a new grandbaby for Christmas." He smiled wryly then shrugged. "And that she's getting her son back, along with a daughter-in-law who he loves more than life itself."

She hugged him, so proud of how far Dirk had come. "Your family is going to be so excited to see you."

All her dreams were coming true. She was getting a family. Dirk's family. And most importantly, she was getting the man she loved and who loved her. Dirk.

He grinned. "Yeah, and you know what? I'm going to be excited to see them, too, and to see their faces when I hand out their gifts."

"Gifts?" Abby raised her brow in question. "What did you get them?"

"Bought each one of them a *Dummies Guide*

to Holding an Intervention and wrote a message, letting them know how much I appreciate them and that they have my permission to intervene anytime deemed necessary."

Abby laughed. "Oh, Dirk, you really are serious about this, aren't you?"

His brow lifted. "Did you doubt me?"

Had she? No, she trusted him with her heart, with their baby's heart. He loved them. She could see that truth in his eyes, feel it in his touch, in the way he'd cherished her while they'd made love. "Not in the slightest. You're a good man."

"I'm your man, Abby." He smiled in a way that reached in and touched her very being. "I'll always be your man. Merry Christmas, sweetheart."

"The best." But she suspected only the beginning of even happier times when she and Dirk celebrated the holidays with their baby, with his family—their family. "Merry Christmas to you, too. You've given me so much."

"Not nearly as much as you've given me. You gave me back my life, my heart, my family, my belief in Christmas." He placed his palm over her belly, caressing her there. "I love you and our baby."

Knowing Dirk had made her Christmas dreams come true, would continue to make them come true every day for the rest of their lives, Abby rolled over to kiss her very own Santa all over again.

MEDICAL™

Large Print

Titles for the next six months…

July

SHEIKH, CHILDREN'S DOCTOR...HUSBAND	Meredith Webber
SIX-WEEK MARRIAGE MIRACLE	Jessica Matthews
RESCUED BY THE DREAMY DOC	Amy Andrews
NAVY OFFICER TO FAMILY MAN	Emily Forbes
ST PIRAN'S: ITALIAN SURGEON, FORBIDDEN BRIDE	Margaret McDonagh
THE BABY WHO STOLE THE DOCTOR'S HEART	Dianne Drake

August

CEDAR BLUFF'S MOST ELIGIBLE BACHELOR	Laura Iding
DOCTOR: DIAMOND IN THE ROUGH	Lucy Clark
BECOMING DR BELLINI'S BRIDE	Joanna Neil
MIDWIFE, MOTHER...ITALIAN'S WIFE	Fiona McArthur
ST PIRAN'S: DAREDEVIL, DOCTOR...DAD!	Anne Fraser
SINGLE DAD'S TRIPLE TROUBLE	Fiona Lowe

September

SUMMER SEASIDE WEDDING	Abigail Gordon
REUNITED: A MIRACLE MARRIAGE	Judy Campbell
THE MAN WITH THE LOCKED AWAY HEART	Melanie Milburne
SOCIALITE...OR NURSE IN A MILLION?	Molly Evans
ST PIRAN'S: THE BROODING HEART SURGEON	Alison Roberts
PLAYBOY DOCTOR TO DOTING DAD	Sue MacKay

MEDICAL™

Large Print

October

TAMING DR TEMPEST	Meredith Webber
THE DOCTOR AND THE DEBUTANTE	Anne Fraser
THE HONOURABLE MAVERICK	Alison Roberts
THE UNSUNG HERO	Alison Roberts
ST PIRAN'S: THE FIREMAN AND NURSE LOVEDAY	Kate Hardy
FROM BROODING BOSS TO ADORING DAD	Dianne Drake

November

HER LITTLE SECRET	Carol Marinelli
THE DOCTOR'S DAMSEL IN DISTRESS	Janice Lynn
THE TAMING OF DR ALEX DRAYCOTT	Joanna Neil
THE MAN BEHIND THE BADGE	Sharon Archer
ST PIRAN'S: TINY MIRACLE TWINS	Maggie Kingsley
MAVERICK IN THE ER	Jessica Matthews

December

FLIRTING WITH THE SOCIETY DOCTOR	Janice Lynn
WHEN ONE NIGHT ISN'T ENOUGH	Wendy S. Marcus
MELTING THE ARGENTINE DOCTOR'S HEART	Meredith Webber
SMALL TOWN MARRIAGE MIRACLE	Jennifer Taylor
ST PIRAN'S: PRINCE ON THE CHILDREN'S WARD	
	Sarah Morgan
HARRY ST CLAIR: ROGUE OR DOCTOR?	Fiona McArthur